STRANGE STONES

HORROR

Strange Stones
Copyright © 2025 by Edward Lee & Mary SanGiovanni
Cover by Joel Amat Güell
ISBN 9781960988416 (paperback)

Troy, NY
CLASH Books
clashbooks.com
Distributed by Consortium.
All rights reserved.

First Edition: 2025
Printed in the United States of America.

Mary dedicates this book to fans of strange and unplumbed universes, both of the mind and of the heart.

"The world is indeed comic,
   but the joke is on mankind."

— H.P. LOVECRAFT

STRANGE STONES

EDWARD LEE

MARY SANGIOVANNI

1

Damn it, Everard thought, up at the podium. *Only ten people?*

The convention was being held at a ritzy hotel in Williamsburg, Virginia, and thus far, it seemed a crowded affair by the busy discussion panels he'd already stuck his head in.

All but THIS discussion panel, he concluded.

The programming manager—Everard already forgot her name, but not her bosom—tapped the microphone for that familiar hollow *thump* that told her it was working, then began, "Welcome everyone, to the Why Lovecraft? panel, and here with us tonight is noted academician and author Professor Robert Everard."

Several members of the lilliputian audience applauded, and Everard nodded with a stiff smile. The manager continued, "Professor Everard is here to promote his new book, *Over-Rated: The Life and Work of H.P. Lovecraft,* and is pleased to hear your comments and answer your questions." The manager's eyes thinned over the paltry crowd. "And I don't have to remind you all to be nice..."

What a dud this is gonna be, Everard thought. *I must've been drunk when I said yes.* He took the microphone and began, "Many of you might be thinking it's the height of stupidity for an author to come to a *horror* convention with the expressed purpose of bad-mouthing who many call the greatest horror writer in history. It's kind of like wearing a Yankees hat at a Red Sox game..."

A few people laughed. *Encouraging,* he thought. "And I'm not here so much to promote my new book" —he held it up; beneath the title was an artist's depiction of a very long-faced Lovecraft wearing a dunce cap— "but to try to level the playing field a bit. Many, many horror authors from Lovecraft's day are unheard of now due to the smothering hype bestowed upon Lovecraft since his death. Arthur Machen, Algernon Blackwood, J. Sheridan Le Fanu, just to name a few. The skillsets of these writers so far surpass that of Lovecraft that it's laughable. Machen gave us *The Great God Pan,* Le Fanu gave us *Carmilla,* Blackwood gave us *The Willows.* But what has Lovecraft given us? Flying crabs and fish-people. It doesn't take much of a glance rearward to see that Lovecraft's most celebrated works are howlingly derivative of other, better authors. So why all this hype? It all goes back to one publisher and one book. The publisher, of course, is Arkham House, that began the commencement of all the pro-Lovecraft hoopla. And the one book is *Mein Kampf*, in which Adolf Hitler described the propaganda vehicle known as the Big Lie—"

Some fat punk in the back blurted, "Really, Professor! You're not comparing Lovecraft to Hitler, are you?"

"Oh, not at all," Everard replied, "though I will point out that there are a few comments in Lovecraft's letters that might be construed as pro-Hitlerian. It was Arkham House that perpetuated the Big Lie in *this* case, and from there a mechanism of critical bandwagonism took off and continues to this day. The tenet is, if you tell a lie big enough and enough times, people will believe it. *That's* why Lovecraft has been raved about for all these decades. It's a big lie that readers have been force-fed by a pro-Lovecraftian syndicate designed to make money."

This was when the fat punk frowned, stood up, and left the room. *Well, fuck him anyway...* Everard smiled. "And no one understands more than me what a hard sell this topic is. Last week, at a convention in Maryland, someone wrote May You Be Food For Cthulhu on my hotel room door in red lipstick. At least, I *hope* it was lipstick."

The audience spared a few chuckles. "Indeed, Lovecraft has a very big bandwagon and a multitude of critics to sing his praise, to *speak* for him. But who speaks for the others, the horror authors of greater skill and more importance who've been swept under the carpet by the all-pervading cult of Lovecraft? Well, I do. I speak for them since they can't speak for themselves. There are two sides to every conversation. Well, that's what my book is about, and that's what *I'm* about. I've been listening to people trumpet Lovecraft's greatness for my entire adult life, and by now I've had it... up to my gills..."

Did one person laugh? Perhaps.

"I just want to help set the record straight. The fact of the matter is, at his very best, Lovecraft was a disheveled hack. He was a charlatan with words whose only good concepts came from other writers."

An attractive blonde a few rows back—wearing a LOVECRAFT IS GOD t-shirt—raised her hand. *Oh, no. Here it comes.* Everard's eyes flicked to her blue-jeaned crotch. *At least she's packing some camel-toe.* "Yes, miss?"

"Aren't you being a little harsh, professor?" the blonde asked with rancor in her expression. "Lovecraft's popularity is undeniable, and very few critics maintain anything close to your negative stance—"

It was impossible for the sexist schmuck to remain dormant in Everard's being. *This ditz has boobs to write home about...*

"Surely, there must be something positive you can say about Lovecraft's contributions to the genre. Can't you at least name one story of his that you find commendable?"

Everard looked blankly at her. "Young lady, I must answer your query with a resolute and unwavering *No...* unless by commendable you mean mediocre."

Two more attendees got up and left.

Wow, Everard thought. *This is going to be a long day...*

2

It wasn't as though Everard were one of those pedantic academics who insisted on using his elevated intellect to go against the mainstream consensus—he was not arbitrary for the mere sake of being arbitrary. But he figured his opinions were as qualified as the next person's, or perhaps more so since he was a professor of literature, and some of the "literary" analysis these days seemed a bit off the mark. Hence, during his off months, he'd taken to writing about the purveyors of classic supernatural fiction, the writers who were true artisans and really had something to say that transcended genre. Writers like M.R. James, Edward Lucas White, and William Hope Hodgson, etc. Everard's first book several years ago had made quite a splash in the high-end horror-fiction circles; it was a powerfully positive look at the work of Flemish writer Jean Ray. The book, in fact, got him his first invitations to conventions all over the country. Everard, not the most social of persons, scarcely knew such things existed; nevertheless, his first summer of the book's release, he found himself being invited as a "special guest" to one convention after another. Free airfare, free room, free dealer's table, plus a formidable fee, all in exchange for his presence, sitting on a few discussion panels, and participating in an interview and Q&A panel.

He enjoyed the scenario quite a bit—suddenly, attention was being paid to him, which wasn't really the case at his teaching post. He got to converse with like-minded horror fans and made respectable side-money by selling signed copies of his book at his dealer's table. There were even some "fringe" bene-fits: occasionally, there were some attractive, spookily dressed young women who took a more concerted interest in him, which led to more than a few sudden trips to the hotel's gift shop to buy condoms. *Damn, these conventions aren't bad at all...*

The same went for his second book, an analysis of the work of the little-remembered Bruno Fischer, whose dozens of pseudonymous novels and hundreds of short stories proved a cornerstone to the genre of the day. This book received even loftier acco-lades from the "weird tale" community, and cemented still more convention invitations, which altogether thrilled him in his otherwise studious and solitary existence.

And what also continued to thrill him was the excess of sexually available women. It was uncanny. Many of these women seemed to gravitate toward the younger novelists and horror movie actors, which made sense—some sort of "groupie" phenomenon, he supposed—but even guests such as himself, in their '40s and '50s, often found themselves approached by attractive female fans whose intent was obvious. *What's the big deal with me?* he remembered thinking after his third night in a row of getting lucky at a convention. Lately, by the end of the conventions, he was too tired to even *think* about further intimate parleys. At any rate, it certainly added some spice to his life and proved quite a confidence builder. *Any of these girls who want me can have me!* Many of them wore wedding rings or else displayed tell-tale tan lines of a wedding ring removed; hence, most were married to husbands with no interest in horror conventions, which turned the assembly into a great big hunting ground for such women looking to play around, and Everard reasoned if they wanted to play around with *him,* he was all too eager to oblige.

But the following year—this year—didn't quite carry the same chord. His newest book was *Over-Rated: The Life and Work of H.P. Lovecraft,* whose sales tanked and whose reviews were mostly negative. Weren't people getting sick of listening to the ceaseless blaring of the Lovecraft trumpet? Everard had clearly misjudged the topic; with all the never-ending hype about Lovecraft, he thought that a book offering an alternate view might garner a lot of interest.

Wrong.

Nobody wanted to hear *anything* negative about Lovecraft. The HPL Bandwagon just kept rolling, right over Everard. *Oh well,* he thought. *You live and learn.* The next book would have to be a positive look at a celebrated author, like E.F. Benson or Brian Keene.

Still, he'd been invited again this time anyway, so... *I might as well make the best of it...*

3

The hour-long discussion slot dragged on and on. By now only three audience members remained, and the programming manager didn't look pleased.

"But, professor, what about Lovecraft's critically lauded poetry?" said one redhead in an EVIL DEAD t-shirt. The shirt was tight enough to make her nipples appear on either side of Ash's head.

"Keep in mind," Everard began, trying hard *not* to stare overtly at her breasts. "Walt Whitman's poetry has been critically lauded as well, but it's still... poorly conceived *poop*. And as for Lovecraft's *poetry*, it's all more an exercise in trying to force words to rhyme in a manner that sounds like Dunsany or Poe. I'm sorry I can't agree with you, miss. Poems about fungous from other planets don't quite hold up against the likes of 'The Raven' and 'A Dream Within a Dream.'"

Everard paused to take a sip of water. *Is this EVER*

going to end? But he still had a few minutes, so onward he must go. "In spite of Lovecraft's rampant popularity, I'm afraid there's much to object to about him. First, he was a racist, an elitist, and a stealer of other people's ideas—that's *not* a hatful of winners, is it? In fact, it's difficult to even identify anything about the man that's remotely admirable. He never worked a job, unless you call scribbling out purple prose a job. He never graduated high school but regularly lied that he did. When in New York, he constantly criticized working-class immigrants when, in truth, it was those same immigrants who built the city he lived in and contributed greatly to its diverse society. Lovecraft himself never contributed to anything tangible. He was, in fact, a selfish, lazy gold-digger. And then there's always Lovecraft's rampant racism, for which history, I regret, has given him a free pass."

Another woman testily raised her hand. *Goddamn,* Everard thought. *It's Tit City on this one.* The breasts beneath her CTHULHU FOR PRESIDENT t-shirt were each easily the size of a baby's head. "Lovecraft had flaws, sure, but he was also an unwitting product of the times and of his upbringing. We shouldn't judge the man's *work* because of the man's attitudes, should we? Isn't that ignorant?"

Everard shrugged. "I beg to point out the falsity of your observation, miss. Lovecraft's *attitudes* couldn't be more intertwined with his *work.* His inexcusable racism exists as a subtext in many of his stories: 'Red Hook,' 'He,' 'Innsmouth,' to name a few. I can think of no author of fiction more reprehensibly racist than

Lovecraft. In this day and age, an author with such repugnant views would be lambasted and run out of business. But not Lovecraft—oh, no—not with his non-stop, money-making bandwagon."

Frowns returned Everard's spiel. He knew he was exaggerating, but if he didn't make his point, he wasn't being honest. *Maybe I should've toned it down a little...* The programming manager was looking at her watch with a smirk.

Everard pointed to another raised hand. It was a skinny kid, clearly infuriated. His t-shirt read I'M DREAMING OF A WHITE DOOMSDAY. "What about the Cthulhu Mythos!" he nearly yelled. "You're completely ignoring its importance in modern entertainment. Not just fiction but movies, comics, video games, strategy games. Lovecraft created another *dimension* of horror for his readership; you can't name a more powerful and original fictional universe than the Mythos."

"Oh, but I can, I assure you," Everard replied, looking back at the red-head's burgeoning breasts. "Many far more creative and original worlds were given to us by H.G. Wells, Lewis Carrol, Algernon Blackwood, William Hope Hodgson—and that's just a handful. This haphazard construction of Lovecraft's rips off a good deal of its functionality from Greek and Mesopotamian lore; I'd hardly call *that* original. Ladies and gentlemen, the so-called Cthulhu Mythos is nothing more than a seafood market from outer space—"

"You know something, *professor?*" said the kid. "You *suck.*"

"Young man, that may well be the case," Everard replied, amused. "But there's one person who sucks more. Howard Philips Lovecraft."

With that, the programming manager stood up and interrupted as quickly as she could, "Professor Everard, I'm afraid our time is up, but thank you for your little talk," and then she addressed the few audience members who remained. "Thank you for coming, everybody, and please join us for our next panel, When Is Extreme Horror Too Extreme?"

Shit, Everard thought. *I've had nightmares that went better than that.* Panelists and audience members for the next event began to sweep into the room. Everard, out of some obligation, felt it necessary to address the programming manager. "Thanks very much for the opportunity. I'm sorry this didn't turn out well"—he chuckled to himself— "Next time I'll be sure to come armed with a more popular topic."

"Yes, yes," she said quickly and shuffled away, with a look in her eyes that suggested *There won't be a next time...*

Everard dawdled at the podium, collecting his books and notes. He spotted a woman sitting in the room's far corner, long jet-black hair, a black fishnet top revealing formidable cleavage, and a long black satiny skirt falling over shapely hips.

Everard hadn't noticed her before.

She looked very witchy, but strikingly so. *Holy shit, how did I miss her? She's the hottest woman I've seen so far, and... Is she? Could she be—*

She stood up and began walking toward Everard. Once arrived, she smiled tersely and said, "Your bravado is admirable, professor." Her voice was low, cool, spooky. "Pushing an anti-Lovecraft book at a horror convention requires some courage."

"And some stupidity, I'm afraid," Everard said. "Perhaps I'm subconsciously a masochist. But at least the audience forgot to bring rotten eggs and tomatoes."

The woman smiled, and from her black bag withdrew a copy of his book. "Would you sign this for me please?"

Everard was nearly flabbergasted when she handed him a copy. He fumbled for a pen. "It would be my pleasure! What's your name?"

"Asenath," she said.

"For real?" Everard exclaimed. "Like the character in 'Thing at the Doorstep?'"

"The same. And it really is my name."

Everard signed the book and returned it. At once he felt magnetized by her presence. The meticulous emerald-green eye-makeup augmented eyes the same exact color, bordered by razor-sharp black eyeliner. Her skin was lambent-white, and she had the high cheekbones of a fashion model. Black lipstick, of course, and a black choker about her neck, centered by a black rose. Rings on each white finger sported unusual semi-precious gemstones, which made her hands flash and wink like some otherworldly glitter. A fragrant soap-scent or perfume drifted from her to him, which Everard found intoxicating. Her exotic beauty was beginning to stall his thoughts to awkwardness. "And I must say, not only is your costume exquisite, but it couldn't be more appropriate for a forum such as this."

She put her book away and smiled thinly. "Maybe it's not a costume. Maybe I'm really a witch."

"Then that would make you even more inter- esting than you already are." Her arousing beauty was bending him up; he felt on the verge of babbling. "Really, Asenath. We *must* continue our conversation. Meeting you has been the only good thing to happen to me since the convention started. Allow me to buy you a drink at the bar."

Her eyes fixed on him, and she took a breath. "I can't," she told him—

Fuck! Everard thought like a two-by-four snapping.

"But please ask again sometime," she continued, then she gave him her business card. "Right now, I have to get back to my table. Stop by if you're inclined."

I'm fuckin' inclined all right! "Yes, yes, of course, I'll see you soon—"

Everard stood there like a wide-eyed mannequin and watched her disappear through the crowd.

4

He didn't want to go to her table right away; that might seem overzealous, and since no one was buying his new book, he didn't bother returning to his own table. But the merchant's room was fascinating and huge—it looked like at least a hundred tables and dealers selling everything from horror books, obscure DVDs and VHS tapes, comics, t-shirts, knickknacks, cosplay apparel, etc. Everard frowned when he noticed that quite a few tables were chiefly dedicated to Lovecraft. Cthulhu this, Yog-Sothoth that. *I can't get away from the son of a bitch,* he realized. Here was something like a velvet Elvis painting, only it was Lovecraft. Statuettes of King David but with Lovecraft's head. *You gotta be shitting me...* The Lovecraft bobbleheads were Everard's last straw. *No Poe? No Mary Shelley? It's a Lovecraft conspiracy!* He wended quickly out of the sprawling crowd, but even at the exit doors were life-size cardboard cut-outs of Lovecraft, and when he looked inadvertently up, a giant parade-style float hovered there.

Of Lovecraft.

He rushed to the bar—which to his relief wasn't crowded—and ordered a drink. Ordinarily, the shapely barmaid's physique would've spurred his sexist inclinations, but not this one, not with her shirt that read NEVER LET MI-GO. Everard bristled. *It never ends...*

But now he could get his mind off the less-than-positive things. For him, the convention was a bust. He'd sold hardly any books, and he'd learned the hard way never to utter a negative peep about H.P. Lovecraft. *Fuck me...* But next, he took out the business card Asenath had given him. It read, ASENATH'S WITHCRAFT SHACK: GEMS, REGLIA, SPELLBOOKS, POTIONS. The upper left corner had a P.O. Box, a website, and a phone number. Tiny bats and haunted houses decorated the card, along with a caricature sketch of Asenath's face, which only reinforced his memory of her cryptic good looks. The low-cut black top demonstrated a superlative, lily-white cleavage, and this only begged him to imagine what her bare breasts must be like. And in the next blink, he pictured her standing nude right in front of him, smiling ever-so-slightly, and her blazing green eyes seeming to turn kaleidoscopically, and some energy nearly psychic forced his own eyes to pan up and down her exquisite white body. At last, he reimagined that intoxicating fragrance drifting off her. *Fuck,* he thought. He was suddenly hard in his pants, his heartbeat rising.

He couldn't wait any longer; he didn't even finish his drink. It was time to return to the din of the dealer's room and find Asenath...

5

And find her, he did.

She was beautiful sitting behind a long fold-out table in the dealers' room. The table was decked out in suitably witchy décor, with a black banner bearing the name on her business card draped over the table to obscure her legs. On one end of the table sat a silver tray with small boxes marked CHOCO-LATE: PUMPKINS, CHOCOLATE: BATS, CHOCO-LATE: SKULLS, and little pictures on the labels of the contents within. Near the boxes, bottles filled with clear or brown liquid had been labeled as potions of different kinds, with a little bat and the store logo in each of the top corners. In the center of the table, a small stack of her business cards sat. To its left was a display of palm-sized crystals. To its right, tiny seal-able bags with different shades of dull green plant matter—herbs, by the look of their labels—were laid out next to long, thin boxes of incense. At the end of the table, a leafless black tree, probably plastic and about two feet tall, reached outward with spindly branches bearing silver rings with spiders and webs, triple moons, pentagrams, triquetras, fertility goddesses, and the like. *Costume jewelry*, he thought. *Cheap nonsense, easily digestible by the uninitiated but curious, those looking for a little occult thrill without the knowledge to wield it.* Everard knew a little about witchcraft, particularly where its mythologies and rituals blended into Machen's, Blackwood's, and Lovecraft's work. He didn't think much of its efficacy—no more than he thought of Lovecraft's writing, truth be told—but if feigning interest and browsing Asenath's wares brought him any closer to seeing what that body looked like under all the fishnet, well hell, he'd change his religion.

As he approached the table, she smiled at him, a sly turn of those slightly parted red lips. Blue eyes looked him up and down in a surprisingly salacious way. Somewhere in the back of his mind, he thought, *Weren't her eyes green?* But then the thought vanished, and he was, in fact, looking into green eyes, and unsure how he had thought they had been blue.

"Hi," he said, smiling. For a moment, she didn't speak, didn't return the greeting. The moment stretched until he began to feel awkward and sucked in a breath to speak again. Before he could, she winked at him and spoke.

"Well, professor. A pleasant surprise."

"I, uh, I thought I'd come by. You know, check out what you've got. On your table, I mean. Check out your..." he gestured at the table, feeling a flush rise in his face.

At first, Asenath did nothing to rescue him from his bumbling attempts at conversation. The look in her eyes—they were definitely green—was one of amusement and maybe something else. *Interest? Could she actually be interested in me?*

He tried hard not to take an eye-dive into that cleavage. He had a good view of it from where he stood. In fact, as she leaned an elbow on the table, the neckline of her top shifted, and he thought he caught a glimpse of her nipple before her voice drew his gaze upward again.

"Hungry?"

For a moment, he was sure she'd read his thoughts. "I'm sorry?"

"I saw you looking at the chocolate," she replied, reaching under the table and pulling out a pale-yellow chocolate box, open to display an arrangement of miniature Cthulhus, Wilbur Whatelys, a decrepit house—presumably The Shunned House—in dark, milk, and white chocolate. "I just made these. You'll probably find them amusing." She popped a white Shunned House into her mouth, and her captivating smile reappeared.

Everard chuckled to himself. Every-fucking-where, Lovecraft was. "I've no choice but to consume Cthulhu. Ia, ftagn, eh?" His hand hovered over a dark chocolate mini-monstrosity. "How much?"

"For you, professor?" She titled her head coquettishly. "On the house. Try one, if you're interested. I promise you, it'll melt in your mouth."

He felt a stir in his pants again. Reaching for the dark chocolate piece, he said, "I think the dealers' room closes at 7 tonight." He popped the chocolate into his mouth, and it was *good*—so good that he felt warm all over and actually, a little tingly. It was a pleasant sensation. He lost himself for a fraction of a second. Asenath was not only hot, but a damn fine chocolatier, as well.

The world came back into focus, though, when he swallowed. "If you're hungry yourself, maybe we can grab something to eat in the bar? Can't live on chocolate alone, right?" He chuckled at his joke and felt goofy for doing so. *Stupid stupid stu*—

"Hey, professor!"

He turned at the sound of the voice and saw a line of three standing behind him. At the head of the line stood the ostensible owner of the voice, the young man in the I'M DREAMING OF A WHITE DOOMSDAY t-shirt.

"You're holding up the line," the young man said flatly. "Can you creep on her after hours? Some of us want to spend money."

Everard held up his hands in an exaggerated apology as he backed away from the table. To Asenath, he mouthed, "Sorry," and she nodded.

Then she leaned over the table conspiratorially, flashing dangling cleavage. "Find me in the bar later. I have a hell of an appetite." She winked at him again and offered a smile that was downright lewd.

Everard managed to make it just outside the hotel lobby doors before whisper-shouting "Yes!" and pumping his fist in victory. A few con-goers milling around the designated smoking area gave him quizzical looks, but he ignored them.

The cool air felt good on his face as he walked. He'd been starting to feel really hot in the dealers' room, and only some of the heat had been due to Asenath's proximity. His head felt a little light, too, if he was to be honest.

At the corner, he turned and glanced behind him at the hotel. It was only half a block away, but it looked much farther.

And then closer.

And then much, much farther away. *Too far to walk back before I pass out*, he thought. He looked up at the blue and white street sign and tried to read it, but he had trouble getting the letters to come into focus.

Tremont Street. It blurred.

No, College Street.

The sign blurred again. East Knapp Street. No, that couldn't be right. He blinked hard and tried again.

Federal Hill.

Then suddenly it was Tremont Street again.

He shook his head to clear it, gave his cheek a light slap, and found he could feel neither.

Fuck, he thought. *This is not good. Not good... did she... did she dose me?* And then he remembered the chocolate. *But why?*

As if in answer to his thoughts, his cell phone vibrated. He pulled it from his pants pocket and saw that there were two text notifications from an unknown number. He frowned and tapped on the first.

How are you feeling? ;)

The second one popped up from the same unknown number.

Are you still hot for me?

Asenath—it had to be her. But how had she gotten his number?

The text screen swam in front of him. His head hurt now. The sound around him muted. He glanced up to see a woman walking by, but she had no face. She was pushing a stroller with a baby made of eyes and long, worming tentacles.

He looked away, but his eyes wouldn't focus on anything solid, anything real. All the buildings around him seemed to be slanting, their angles converging and pulling apart while their straight lines ran into impossible nothingness and still kept going.

Everard looked back at his phone and tried to type, but it was nearly impossible to make out the letters.

Wht did u do 2 me

Three little dots rippled across the corner of the screen, indicating she was typing back.

Words appeared.
Potion inside the chocolate. Very effective.

Oh god, she was nuts. Did that say potion, or poison? He couldn't tell. His eyes wouldn't do the work for him.

He felt genuine panic rising from gut to chest. She had poisoned him, potioned him, all the same thing, really, and now he was going to die. Why hadn't he seen it? All these Lovecraft fanatics, they were all crazy, all a Dagon-dick's length waaay off the deep end, and this bitch... this bitch wanted to kill him over some stupid presentation.

He tried to type back: *Y R U doing ths 2 mw?*

For several seconds, there was no indication of a response. Then the three little dots—what he had come to regard as "thinking dots"—appeared, followed a few seconds later by words. He blinked hard, forcing the words into focus.

Because you're a nasty little nutless hack who gets off on bashing the accomplishments of men more talented than you.

At least, that's what he thought it said, in the two or three moments his vision cleared. Then the letters blurred again, and when they reformed, the same message now read:

If you tell a lie big enough and enough times, people will believe it. That's what you said. And you were right... about that. About Lovecraft, you were wrong. He had the power to tap into the

Otherworld, to take what is a truth there and a lie here and make it truth everywhere... the Old Gods gave him that power. He has paved the way to make lies truth.

He managed, or thought he managed, to type back *WTF R U talkin ab*—before the phone melted in his hand.

Hallucination? Or real?

The burn in his palm felt *very* real. He desperately dropped the molten device, shaking his hand hard to dislodge the thick, squirming black fluid that was making an escape up his wrist.

Must be LSD, he considered, still wobbly. Everard had never tried it, but he'd heard it could make for some convincing sights and sounds. *LSD and God knows what else. Just what I need. Boy, did I pick the wrong tit-wagon to lust after...*

Everard stumbled forward and kept stumbling, then kept running until the indistinct sounds of shouting and honking faded and the ground beneath his feet gave some yield. He bent over, sucking in heavy, ragged breaths from the exertion of running, his head pounding, his fists clenched and shaking.

When his breathing and heartbeat finally settled on a calmer rhythm, he straightened and looked around. He was surprised to find that his headache immediately faded to a faint throb, and his vision had cleared entirely. If anything, he saw things even more sharply, more vividly than before.

And he didn't know *what* was going on, but he knew this:

He was not in Williamsburg.

There was nothing like what he was seeing anywhere near the convention hotel. Instead, from the hill he'd just crested, he saw what appeared to be a run-down residential street winding upward, but the architecture was not quite right. Rather than the 18th century colonials for which Williamsburg was so well-known, the street here was lined with homes that appeared much older. Worn steps led to unwelcoming doors, Doric porches stooped beneath the weight of years, and cupolas stared with cataract-blind windows smeared with grime. A dingy blue-and-white street sign told him nothing; the characters squirmed into shapes beyond his comprehension.

He began to climb the strange road's ascent.

About halfway up the incline, he began to breathe harder, noting with dismay that he was getting out of shape. Life on the road did that—eating fast food and hotel food, sleeping poorly, drinking excessively. While it was true that the only exercise he got nowadays was at conventions, in the form of sex with pretty young fans, it was clear to him that letting the girls ride him while he lay on his back was not the cardio workout he'd imagined it was.

He was pulled from these thoughts by the peripheral notice of the foreign signs over brown-brick shops to which the old houses had given way. Where the hell *was* he? There were no people on the street—not one—and the very few cars looked like sagging, faded versions of the specimens at an antique car show. He touched one, and it felt solid enough beneath his fingertips. He had to give Asenath credit; whatever she had dosed him with was high-quality stuff. He could almost believe she'd sent him to another place, another time.

But he had to get out of there. Drugged or not, he had to pull what was left of his senses together, find a phone, and call an Uber or something to take him back to the convention center.

The shops all looked closed—at least, he thought they were closed based on the dark windows and empty doorways. No traffic in or out, and when he cupped his hands around his eyes and peered through a glass storefront into an interior, he saw a dusty counter and half-dressed mannequins, but no people. There was something about the mannequins that put him off; their barely delineated, unpainted faces were placid masks of disquiet, and their unsuited limbs, he saw, were bent at unnatural angles. They could have been contortionist mimes having an animated conversation in slow motion.

He pulled away from the window and shook his head to clear the absurd thought away. Contortionist mimes? Where had *that* come from?

The chocolate, of course. His mind still wasn't quite right, and probably wouldn't be for a while yet.

Still, it was midday on a Saturday afternoon—*late day*, he corrected himself, glancing at the gathering gray in the sky—and some business somewhere had to be open. He just had to keep looking.

He was watching at his feet, cursing the steepness of the hill again as he crested it, so it wasn't until the road leveled off that Everard looked up and saw that he stood in an empty cobblestone square, at the foot of massive stone steps climbing toward a padlocked gate. Rising above that, severe and at once unsettling in its imposing architecture, was a church.

Everard stared upward for some time.

It was a massive stone building, nearly a cathedral, really, and might once have been lovely. Now, though, it was a testament to the fading power of religion in its decrepitude. He saw it had once boasted of high stone buttresses, but many of them had fallen, and several of its delicately carved finials lay tangled in the brown, overgrown weeds and grasses. Its large Gothic windows remained mostly intact, the brilliant colors of the glass panes were faded now, so the shapes and scenes they were meant to form were difficult to make out. Many of the stone mullions were cracked or missing altogether.

Fully enclosing the grounds was an iron gate rusted to an ugly orange color. Slivers of black jutted from the iron like coarse hairs, and Everard shivered to imagine one of those slivers embedding itself into the careless hand that dared to touch the gate.

It was then that an oddity struck him, an inner distraction that was somehow linked to this church. Was it déjà vu? Some imagined familiarity? *Shit!* Yes, there *was* something vaguely, even grimly familiar about this gravestone-gray pile of a building, and as he moved on, the thought kept pecking at him.

He climbed the steps and stood just outside the property, taking in the overgrown path from the gate to the building, the birdless eaves, and the black, ivyless walls. Yes, no birds perched on the structure's eaves nor on the ledges of the high bell tower, while there was no shortage of doves, crows, etc., milling about on the eaves of nearby buildings.

That was when the answer came to him, absurd as it might seem.

Oh my God.

He knew this place, all right, although he had never seen it anywhere but in his mind's eye. It was too big, too solid, too *there* to be a figment of drugs or fevered imagination, but... it didn't exist.

That is, it didn't exist outside of a story by a hack weird fiction writer, written as playful banter between the man and a protégé by the name of Bloch.

Inexplicably as it seemed, Everard was staring at the Church of Starry Wisdom, from Lovecraft's own "The Haunter of the Dark."

He glanced around but saw no one. His mouth felt dry, and his head ached.

What the hell is going on? How—

He had to see. There was a hell of a lot he was willing to chalk up to stress and drugs, but this... this was something else. He felt that as surely and completely as he felt the burgeoning superstitious dread at such close proximity to the place.

Maybe I'm insane, he chuckled to himself. He knew only one thing then: he had to get inside.

Everard followed the length of fence to the right, and found a spot where the rust looked least likely to give him tetanus and several bars were missing. He slipped between them to the other side.

On the inside of the property looking out, he wondered if he had made a mistake, like he had climbed into the waiting jaws of a lion. He surveyed the square below, surrounded by the decaying architecture of Lovecraft's degenerate places in Rhode Island and Massachusetts. Everard was looking out over Providence, not Williamsburg.

But that was impossible... wasn't it?

A nagging voice in the back of his mind reminded him of Lovecraft's supposed ties to the occult and its practitioners. It reminded him of the power of words and of suggestion. It was Asenath's text-voice, silent and mocking. *If you tell a lie big enough and enough times, people will believe it.*

And what was reality, anyway, but the lies people told each other it was?

He had the power to tap into the Otherworld...

Everard told himself *no*, but his own inner voice was small and weak. It was hard to argue with a church he could see and touch, the mustiness and age that he could smell.

Slowly, he approached the doors and reached for the handle as if it might be hot to the touch. It was cold, very cold, and it wouldn't budge. The door was locked. He felt a small amount of relief in that.

This close to the edifice he realized its true size, a colossal grime-stained bulk, its stones almost black due to the century-plus of its lofty place here amidst the town extruding wood- and coal-smoke. When he looked up at the highest spire he nearly fell over from dizziness.

The massive front doors had been locked in the story, too, hadn't they? But he felt determined to get inside, no matter what, even if it were all hallucina-

tions, even if he were genuinely mad. *Wait a minute...*
In the story, how did the protagonist, Blake, finally get
into the church? Everard racked his brain, then it hit
him. *A basement window!* But now his disbelief
became tinged with some arcane excitement, and he
waded into the tangled, sickly overgrowth of weeds,
nearly tripping over hidden grave markers. He even
noticed one plot that had recently collapsed,
revealing its ancient, disheveled occupant, or at least
part of it. A skeleton did indeed lay within but a *head-
less* skeleton. Everard didn't want to think for what
purpose the skull had been absconded with.

He continued to crunch his way around the
church until—sure enough—he found a basement
window devoid of glass. It provided an aperture large
enough to admit a grown man. He knelt in the grass,
aware that the cool ground beneath him was inordi-
nately spongy and slippery, and peered into the
yawning opening.

What little light that penetrated the basement
showed only cobwebs and debris. If his phone hadn't
melted, he could've used the flashlight app, but fortu-
nately, Everard—a nerd of the first water—always
carried a penlight, and this he turned on at once and
scanned the narrow white beam across the almost
fathomless expanse of the basement. Everard was not
surprised to see the old barrels, rotting cardboard
boxes, and broken furniture under a grim blanket of
dust, let alone a rusted-out hot-air furnace against
the far wall.

The same exact things that were in the basement in
the story. What next?

After some swearing, he gained entrance, stepping on boxes for leverage. When he stepped down to the floor, one box tipped over and out spilled a dozen mold-splotched copies of *The Book of Common Prayer.* At first he was perplexed as to why these would be down here, but then he recalled that this church had been denounced in the story and would have little use for Christian prayer books. As he entered deeper, he saw more evidence of the same: large brass crucifixes—several of them—lying on the floor beneath the carpet of dust. *That's what I call showing Jesus the door,* Everard thought. Another box was filled with the typical raiment worn by ministers, deacons, and choirists, all discarded and mildewed like trash.

Everard stumbled along, mindful of his steps. Could there be rats in a place like this? Snakes or perhaps black widows? *Fuck this,* he thought, buttoning his sleeves. Something seemed heavy about the darkness; something made him feel he was wearing weighted shoes. That, of course, and the universal feeling of being watched, and he knew that whatever might be observing him was not human. By now, he'd crossed half of the immense black basement, all the while feeling more and more in the confines of some spectral cognizance. Everard—an empiricist—was not afraid of such incorporeal impressions, but he had to admit, just then, that he was shit-scared. More and more the notion trickled into his sentience: he was walking within the solid stone walls of a structure that didn't really exist.

If I don't like it, he reminded himself, *I can leave.*

Now his memory was sharpening; he was

remembering more of Lovecraft's story. *It was his last story, wasn't it?* He felt sure. *Before the poor bastard died of cancer?*

Now, from the story, he remembered the protagonist finding a black stone arch which led up to a corridor on the first floor and, eventually, the nave of the church. And after one more step forward, there it was: the arch and the staircase. Everard felt a striking thrill and lunged forward, but the arch seemed to hang in the cobwebbed darkness.

Do I REALLY want to go up there?

It took a full minute of contemplation to produce his answer. It wasn't that he *wanted* to go up there. He simply *had* to.

Don't be a pussy, he told himself, mounting the steps. Each footfall echoed loudly all through the basement and up the stairwell, such that if anyone was there, they'd know he was coming. Next, at the top, came the latched door that opened inward, and through that, the barely lit corridor lined by paneling filled with wormholes. *Think, think!* He ordered himself. *What did Blake do next in the damn story?* A row of doors lined the hallway, and after peeking into a few, he concluded, just as the character had, that the rooms were of little interest. But then he found himself in the overlarge nave and its rows and rows of box-pews.

He reached into one and withdrew a prayer book, thumbed through its pages, and blanched. If these were prayers, they were in no language Everard could identify, more like twisted and demented hieroglyphs, and the print was in scarlet ink, not black.

The endpapers depicted some lifeform completely disparate from the planet Earth, a gelatinous thing standing upright on three jointless legs and possessed of tentacular arms. Its body seemed comprised of warped globes or jellyfish nodes of some kind, and within each globe hung particulate fragments of light and repulsive wormlike threads. The creature's own genetic nature had left it with a halved head whose crevasse burned more wormlike filaments, reminiscent of antennae. There was no face, no eyes, and no mouth, but hanging betwixt the tripod of legs was indeed something that could only be a sex organ, plump and feet-long, connected at some modicum of "groin" around which hung testicles the size of grapefruits.

This monstrosity, Everard supposed, was some manner of Shoggoth.

He flung the book away, nauseous. A glance upward showed him a vaulted ceiling whose ornate beauty was besmirched by garlands of rope-thick cobwebs. He meant to proceed next to the chancel but then recalled from the story how Blake had stumbled upon several apses which displayed obscured but intact stained-glass windows. Mostly blood-red light filtered in through the leaded glass, and painted on the panes were scenes that clearly contradicted Christian artistic tradition. One bearded man with a face stretched by agony was buried up to his neck as an armored soldier in a pointed basinet helm was yanking his scalp off with iron tongs. Another window showed a group of villagers grinning as naked children were thrown into a roaring fire.

Another: a comely nude woman staked spread-eagled to the ground. She was being raped by some abomination similar to the creature on the endpapers, but then... how could it be rape when the woman had ecstasy in her eyes? Around the spectacle stood hooded figures garbed in orange and scarlet cloaks, and all were holding up sparkling objects akin to variously sized gemstones of varying colors. One of these gems, displayed by a central figure, shined somehow blackly with glowing red striations. This, Everard knew, was the story's keynote feature: the otherworldly and madness-inducing Shining Trapezohedron.

Oh, yuck! He thought when he looked at the next window. This one showed a nun being bisected from crotch to head by villagers with hewers, and another showed piles of severed heads in a field, and next to it a pile of something else that Everard refused to speculate upon.

The last window he would look at offered a black void whose limits seemed to expand past the physical limits of the pane and in which helixes of flecks of light seemed to spin multi-dimensionally. For sure, this illusion was the work of a highly skilled artist.

The windows were giving him a headache, so he trudged away from the apses and moved up the chancel. At least an inch of undisturbed dust carpeted his way; gray puffs billowed up with each step forward. But at least he could see more up here from the slants of daylight streaming in through the stained glass.

He traversed the chancel, the choir seats, and the

sounding board and then noticed, suspended above the altar itself, exactly as retailed in the story, not the conventional cross one might expect but the arcane and very occult-looking ankh-style cross. No messiah, no sons of any gods, had anything to do with this sort of cross, for it was at least three thousand years older than Christianity. The teardrop shaped loop at the top was thought to be a doorway to either the afterlife or infinity.

Everard inadvertently walked behind the altar into the presbytery but was immediately compelled to leave, almost via an invisible act of violence. *Damn! Did something just SHOVE me away?* He wondered, agitated. *Something doesn't want me there...* He couldn't help but think of Lovecraft's "Diary of Alonzo Typer," where invisible paws tried to push Mr. Typer down the stairs of a haunted house...

He couldn't have left the presbytery in more haste. *Time to get down to business,* he knew. He needed to get to the high tower room and, if possible, the windowless steeple compartment at the very top. He easily remembered the spiral stairs that Blake found in the tale; they were behind a door on the side vestibule. Everard turned, saw the door, and entered it, again wielding his penlight. It was indeed a spiral staircase he ascended, which provided periodic windows through which he could see for quite a distance. *Yeah, I'm fucked,* he thought miserably when, even from this height, he recognized no sign of the Williamsburg tourist district and no sign of the fifteen-story convention hotel.

Hallucination or not, the only thing to do was

continue his mission as if the church was real. If this was the result of a spell that Asenath had put on him, or some supernatural potion, what could he possibly do about? *If I only had my cellphone, I could call the bitch,* he thought futilely. *To hell with it. Just keep going...*

Up the spiral staircase he continued, and finally, after some huffing and puffing, he reached the terminus of the wooden steps, facing a narrow door. *This should lead to the tower chamber,* he told himself. *Let's see how long this hallucination replicates the descriptive components of the story.* In most churches, the tower room would be a bell tower but in "The Haunter of the Dark," it wasn't.

He opened the door, which gave off an appropriate creak. *So far the hallucination, or whatever this is, is batting a thousand.* He stepped into four blocks of late-afternoon light beaming in through the four louvered windows. The room seemed to exist for the benefit of the four-foot-high pillar erected in the center of it. Around this pillar stood seven carven-backed chairs, all surrounding a substantial dust-cloaked lump in the pillar's center. But Everard knew exactly what the dust-covered lump was, and he couldn't believe he was actually looking at it—

There it is, he thought. *The true star of Lovecraft's final piece of fiction, the Shining Trapezohedron...*

Dirtying his hands was unavoidable as he brushed inches of dust off the four-inch-wide stone as well as its metallic gold box or perch. Well, no, it *had* to be a box, he remembered, because it had a lid that was now standing open, displaying the polyhedron to anyone in proximity. The stone's bulk fascinated Everard—shiny as polished glass and blacker than any shade of black he'd ever envisioned in life. His fingers on it detected warmth, or at least he thought so, and when the warmth seemed to abate, the crazily-angled jewel actually seemed to *beat.*

Almost akin to a heart.

Still following the nearly century-old story, red striations marbled the stone like threads that seemed possessed of their own luminosity. It was strangely beautiful even as the threads were so thin as to be nearly imperceptible. It was then that he winced to himself and remembered the story's most dire rules.

NEVER stare into the stone, and NEVER close the lid on the box...

Closing the lid would only submerge the Trapezohedron into darkness and thus enliven what it was that aboded either in the church or in the stone itself. Perhaps a similar shroud of darkness sent a summons through the stone, which in turn communicated and then activated the so-called darkness-thriving Haunter. If Everard remembered the story precisely enough, that Haunter might be as close as the windowless steeple-room just above his head.

Everard looked upward, noticing the old trapdoor in the ceiling and the old wooden ladder built into the side-wall.

Am I really going to go up there? He asked himself.

But he also recalled that simply *staring* into the stone could show the viewer impossible dimensions and non-terrestrial plains on which had been built equally impossible cities. Such cities were constructed out of shuddering geometric structures all webbed by the same sorts of striations that crawled all over the stone.

And there was one more reason not to stare into the stone, no matter how irresistible the desire. Along with cosmic scenery, it would deliver *insanity* to whichever viewer might stare at it too long.

Note to self. Don't stare at the motherfuckin' stone...

One thing he *could* stare at, though, was the yellow metal box the stone sat in, as well as the opened lid. Both displayed intricate engravings and outlandish bas-reliefs: a tableau of unworldly monsterdom and horrid, freezing terrascapes. Everard knew it must be eyestrain, but the creatures that were represented—much more ghastly than the Shoggoth in the prayer book—seemed to move infinitesimally, while several seemed to urge themselves forward, enlarging themselves on the shining metal, moving in and out of perspective. Others, too, seemed overtly *aware* of him. Was one even reaching out with multi-knuckled, two fingered hands? Spiral shapes like those downstairs in the glass were more apparent here, more dimensional, and more suggestive of actual depth and movement. Warped pictograms and glyphic etchings covered more of the box and also traveled down the pillar itself.

Everard felt gross by now; he was sweating, and the hovering dust was sticking to him. He sat down, frustrated, in one of the high-backed chairs and realized, *Fuck. I need a drink.* He couldn't shed his worries. If his seeing things had been the result of poison, how long would it last, and if he'd been hexed, when would it wear off? Was Asenath malicious enough to imprison him here forever? *Fuck this shit,* he thought as profanely as he could manage. *All this shit because I wanted a piece of ass. Talk about Hell Hath No Fury... the BITCH.* But of course, he still didn't know what this really was: it could be madness, a nightmare, some sort of schizo-affectiveness, or even a psychotic break. All he could do, he supposed, was wait and see...

He kept looking at the yellow metal box. Not every detail of Lovecraft's story could he remember, but he knew the metal that comprised the box was not gold. It was something else, something precious from someplace far removed from the earth, and so was the Shining Trapezohedron. It had been brought here by some corrupt agency or endeavor, over a million years ago, perhaps much longer. Evidently, in 1844, an archaeologist had found the box and stone at a dig in Egypt, then had brought it to Providence and bought this abandoned church as a place to store the stone, worship its powers, and start a congregation. This was when the church had undergone a name-change, from the Free Will Church to—

The Church of Starry Wisdom, Everard finished. That was when all the trouble began. Disappearances of adults AND children. Evidence of rampant, grisly violence, body parts found butchered, curiously burned, and even partially eaten or found without a trace of blood.

Everard could see through the louver slats that daylight was dwindling; one place he didn't want to be after dark was an antechamber for a para-dimensional creature that thrived in darkness. He got up, walked to the door to the stairs down, opened it—

"Holy motherfuckin' SHIT!" he bellowed. "You gotta be fuckin' SHITTING me!"

A tall man was standing right in front of the doorway, as if about to enter himself, and he seemed nearly as shocked as Everard. "Sorry if I gave you a start," said the man in a trace New England accent. "If it's any consolation, you gave me one as well."

"GodDAMN, you scared the shit out of me," Everard replied, his heart actually skipping beats. "I didn't think anyone was here."

"Nor did I, and I suppose I have no right to ask what you're doing here, because we both seem to be trespassers; judging by your rather... idiosyncratic apparel, I take it you're *not* a custodian or a member of the congregation."

"You definitely got that right," Everard said, having regained his breath. "I'm no good with a mop and I've never been a member of *any* church. I'm just..." but here his response hit a dead-end. *What can I say, for pity's sake? I ate a chocolate bat made by a witch with big tits, and next thing I know, I'm here?* Instead, he simply offered his hand. "I'm Robert Everard, and I'm just sort of investigating things. I'm quite interested in the architecture of the Gothic Revival period."

The man shook Everard's hand. "Well, you might say I'm on an investigation myself. I'm Ed Lillibridge. I'm chasing down a lead for the *Providence Telegram.*"

Everard tensed at the man's name. *In the story, Blake found the corpse of a reporter named Lillibridge, decomposed to bones and shreds of clothing, in this very room.* Now the reason for the man's outdated clothing —a long-tailed frock coat with overlarge buttons— made more sense. The same man who was mauled to death in this room in 1893 by none other than the Haunter of the Dark...

"Are you aware of the rumors about this church?" Lillibridge asked.

Everard saw no harm in having out with it. "Renamed the Church of Starry Wisdom in 1844 and founded by an archaeologist named Enoch Bowen."

"More than an archaeologist," Lillibridge added. "Also, an occultist, an astrologer, and a medium."

Everard smiled. "Do you believe in things like that? The supernatural, I mean."

"No, Mr. Everard, I most emphatically do *not*. But I *do* believe that certain *people* believe it when convinced by a leader smart enough and charismatic enough. Men like that can have people believing anything."

"Fair enough," Everard agreed. He was going to cite Hitler as a prime example, but then it occurred to him: *Lillibridge doesn't even know who Hitler is; he hasn't even been born.*

"This is interesting," the newspaperman continued. "I mean, that you should be familiar with the story. It was very hushed up when it all came to a head, and that was almost twenty years ago. I was just a kid."

"Weren't there a few death-bed confessions?" Everard seemed to remember from Lovecraft's yarn. "People admitting to perpetrating murders and sacrifices? Even being allowed to glimpse other inter-dimensional realms?"

Lillibridge's brows rose. "I'm impressed. I assumed all those details were forgotten by now. Well, then, tell me this since you know so much. What mythic totem served as the congregation's object of worship?"

Everard shrugged. "The Shining Trapezohedron."

Lillibridge paused, wide-eyed. "How on *earth* do you know about *that?*"

If I told l you, you'd think I was insane, whether you really exist or not. "Let's just say I'm smarter than I look. And I've got news for you. The Shining Trapezohedron isn't mythic. It's real."

Now Lillibridge looked struck. But that's preposterous. It was simply an invention used to beguile a gullible congregation."

"Oh, it's real all right. In fact, it's no farther away than a few steps behind me," and then Everard stepped aside and let Lillibridge enter the dusty louvered chamber.

"I-I can't believe what I'm seeing," Lillibridge croaked. "It's exactly as described by the witnesses. But I never imagined it could look so stunning..."

Everard came in casually behind him. "Yes, it's quite a sight, isn't it? Its asymmetry is fascinating; it looks warped but the points on each end seem to form a perfect axis."

Lillibridge didn't seem to hear him; he was leaning over, hands on knees, and focusing his stare down into the stone's black depths.

Oops! Everard rushed forward, grabbed Lillibridge's shoulders and pulled him back, severing his focused stare. "I forgot to tell you. Rule Number One. NEVER stare into the stone."

Lillibridge was flustered. "Whyever not?"

"Well, because it can transport you to other dimensions and make you stark-raving mad, and that's just for starters. But go ahead and touch it a moment. It's warm. It beats like a heart."

"You're right!" Lillibridge exclaimed, a shaking hand on the multifaceted surface. "That's NOT POSSIBLE. It's obviously solid crystal! How can it beat like that?"

Everard shook his head. "Whatever the reason, I suspect the *human* mind isn't sophisticated enough to comprehend it—that is if you believe in the history of the stone, which you've said you don't."

Lillibridge smiled tersely. "I don't, that's correct. But it is intriguing." Now he turned to face Everard. "But I'm still not quite sure how *you* might fit into all of this..."

Everard considered any possible response. *Should I tell him that he's going to be killed by the Haunter of the Dark? In this very room?* No, he didn't like the prospect of that. But then, what *difference* did it make? Why should he care if Lillibridge thought him insane?

"How I fit in," Everard said. "Well, I could try telling you if you like."

Lillibridge addressed Everard more directly. "By all means."

"I can guarantee you won't believe me, but promise to do me this one favor and just consider it, all right?"

"All right. Please, say on."

Here goes... "I'm from the future." He waited for effect, but at least Lillibridge's expression had not turned to one of hilarity yet. "This is, what? 1893?"

Lillibridge nodded.

"I was transported here by... some mode of occult science instigated by a practitioner whom... I offended. That's about the only way I can put it, so... let's leave it at that for now."

Lillibridge's expression was now changing from one of patience to a tightening smirk of disbelief. Eventually he said, "Okay, Mr. Everard. If what you say is true, what year are *you* from?"

"2024, and I'll prove it." Everard whipped out his wallet and started handing over cards. "That's my driver's license. Note the photo of me and the date."

"A *driver's* license?" Lillibridge asked. "What's that?"

Shit. Did they not have cars here in 1893? "You know, cars, automobiles?"

"Oh," Lillibridge seemed to latch onto some vague familiarity. "Like those motor-wagons I've read that they have in Germany. They say they'll make horses obsolete. Have you ever heard anything so absurd?"

Buddy, you have no idea, Everard thought. "That's my Sunoco card," he said of the next card Lillibridge looked at.

"Suuun-O—"

Never mind. He doesn't know what a fucking gas station is. "Here, this you should find interesting," and he handed the newspaperman a twenty-dollar bill.

Lillibridge squinted carefully at the note. "Well, I'll give you that; it does say 2024. But I can't say Jackson is a favorite of mine, and who on earth is Janet Yellen?"

"She's the Secretary of the Treasury—"

"And how can you expect me to believe *that?*" Lillibridge said testily. "They would *never* give important posts like that to *women.*"

Everard wanted to laugh. *Buddy, you have no idea.*

"Now I suppose you're going to tell me that the women of your time have the right to vote—"

"Not till 1920," Everard enlightened the man. "Not long after World War I."

"World War... *what?*"

"Come on, man!" Everard yelled. "Time's wasting. Do you believe me or not? Fuck, I just showed you stuff from the twenty-first century! What? You think this is some kind of trick to fool you? You think I counterfeited that stuff?"

Lillibridge stroked his chin as though he had a goatee. "Well, if that's the case, it seems to be a very elaborate trick and... it wouldn't make any sense anyway. You don't know me, and I can't imagine how you might profit by making me think you're from the future."

"Eureka!" Everard celebrated. "Now we're getting somewhere! You *do* believe me!"

"Well, I didn't quite say that, but you know..." Lillibridge reached into a jacket pocket. "All this talk of people from the future, I found the strangest object downstairs in one of the vestry rooms. I can't imagine what it is, but it appears to be some sort of device or apparatus, and if anything I've seen today looks like it's from the future, it's this."

"Really?" Everard held out his hand. "Lemme see."

It was something small and black that Lillibridge placed in Everard's hand.

"Holy fuckin' shit!" Everard yelled in a thrill. The object was a cellphone. *Not mine, but who cares?* And it still had over half a charge. "I can't fuckin' believe this fuckin' shit!"

Lillibridge's expression of disapproval couldn't have been more plain. "Your language really is disgraceful, I must say, and there's no call for it. You sound like the men from the shipyards. But, you seem to know what this object is."

"It's called a cellphone. It's like a telephone but without wires. You have telephones, right?"

"Of course! We're not prehistoric here," Lillibridge said. "You seem quite enthused about this —cellphone."

"I am. And you say you found it downstairs?"

"Yes, in a vestry room, in a desk. There were quite a few others with it."

Everard knew he'd have to inspect the other phones, and search for any other items that might be not of this time period.

"The Starry Wisdom congregation," Lillibridge informed, "grew to over two hundred members, but the town council and police ran them out of town, and the church was closed in—"

"1877," Everard remembered from the story.

Lillibridge gave Everard his most suspicious look

yet. "Yes, and it may well be that you and I are the first people to set foot here since then... I must admit, our meeting and this little venture is getting quite interesting."

Everard couldn't resist. "It might get even *more* interesting soon enough." *Like when you're murdered in this room by some phantasmal monster that will melt your bones and bore a hole in your skull. How's that for interesting?*

"Since you seem to be in the know," Lillibridge continued, looking upward at the trapdoor in the ceiling. "Have you any idea what's up there?"

"Yeah. A world of hurt. An *ass*-kicking. Take my word for it. DON'T go up there." Everard figured there was only one thing most logical to try next. He took out Asenath's business card that had her phone number on it. "I wonder what'll happen if I—"

Lillibridge was stooped over, examining the bas-reliefs on the sides of the trapezohedron's box, with some distaste. "Absolutely ghastly, these engravings. But what's that you were saying?"

Everard snorted a laugh. *I'm gonna try to call a real living person in a real place... from what's probably a hallucination. Why not?*

He dialed Asenath's number on the cellphone. It only rang once before it was picked up.

"It took you long enough," Asenath's slow, witchy voice answered.

"Look, I'm sorry!" he blurted, "and I really mean it. I'm sorry I bad-mouthed Lovecraft—believe me, I'm seeing first-hand just exactly what a genius he was. So, all those books he wrote were actually real?

The Necronomicon, the *Pnakotic Manuscripts, Unaussprechlichen Kulten,* and all the rest? All the esoterica, the non-Euclidean geometry, the math-based witchcraft? All that shit really works?"

"How can you not know? You're standing in the middle of it all, aren't you? All that *shit* really works because Lovecraft's mind *made* it work."

Fuck. He scratched his head. "All because of what you put in that damn chocolate bat?"

"A high and mighty elixir," she laughed. "Like Shakespeare said, 'There's more in Heaven and earth,' right? There's also more in the abysms of the cosmos, and in the incogitable horrors we've yet to perceive." She paused. "So, you saying you're *sorry?*"

"Yes, yes, I'm sorry! I'm an arrogant asshole, I admit it," Everard couldn't speak fast enough. "I'm a pedant, an egoist, and a know-it-all—"

"And a sexist cockhound piece of shit who only views women as gravy boats to fill up with their cum?"

Everard frowned. *That's a bit harsh, isn't it?* "Yes, yes! You're right! I took you for granted, I lusted after you, I viewed you as an arrangement of sexual parts, and I'm sorry! I mean, what guy wouldn't? You're so goddamn good-looking I couldn't help it."

"Oh, how sweet," she mocked. "Don't dig your grave deeper by patronizing me. It won't work. Oh, and where are you, by the way? Exham? The Gilman Hotel?"

"At Starry Wisdom Church," Everard croaked. "It exists exactly as it does in the story. I'm even here with Edwin Lillibridge."

Asenath sounded amused. "The poor hack doesn't even know he's dead meat. I wouldn't get too close to him. Otherwise, there'll be *two* melted skeletons that Blake finds."

Everard disregarded the warning. "Lillibridge said he found this cellphone somewhere downstairs, and he said there were *other* cellphones down there too. That tells me you've been sending people here, right? You've been sending them here from there. Why?"

"Well, surely pond-scum like you has heard the term 'A pussy needs to eat.' Well, so does the avatar of Nyarlathotep."

Jesus. Food? It's got to be more than that. "So where are they then? The other people you've sent here? Are they dead?"

"Most of them, of course. But I'd guess a few are still wandering around out there. It's quite an interesting netherscape you've stumbled upon. You could say that, like the Shining Trapezohedron, it's *multifaceted.* Unless you're a lot dumber than I think, you'll find out soon enough."

Everard had no clue what she might be talking about. *She's an occult ho-bag but she knows her shit. Whatever she put in the chocolate can send people to other planes of existence. It's a power that can convert someone's imagination into reality, or maybe... other realities into someone's imagination—LOVECRAFT'S imagination.*

Asenath's voice floated back onto the line. "Remember, now, if you tell a lie big enough and enough times, people will believe it. That's what YOU said. And you were right... about that. About Lovecraft, you were wrong. He had the power to tap into the Otherworld, to take what is a truth there and a lie here and make it truth everywhere... the Old Gods gave him that power. He has paved the way to make lies truth. I'd suggest you think about that very hard, *Professor* Everard. Consider all of the statement's... *facets*—no pun intended. And do you want to know what the biggest surprise is?"

"Yes!" he barked.

"Are you *sure?*

"Yes!"

"Say pretty please with a cherry on top."

"Oh, for fuck's sake! Pretty please with a fuckin' cherry on top!"

A pause. "Okay. The biggest surprise is—"

She hung up.

Everard roared. "Why that iniquitous man-hating *cunt!* I'll kick her right in her fishy innsmouth!" He tried to redial, but of course there was no connection now.

Lillibridge looked at him with a scowl. "I'm sorry to see that the English language has only *de*volved by the time it gets to *your* time."

In spite of it being close to sundown now, the molten light of dusk poured into the room through the louvres. It was very bright but then quickly darkened as clouds moved across the sun. Shadows crept across the floor. "I'm going downstairs to check out the other cellphones."

"All right," Lillibridge said. "I'll be down shortly."

"And remember Rule Number One—"

"Yes. Don't look into the stone."

Everard nodded, turned, then started down the steps, but he didn't get far when an oversight occurred to him as well, so he called back, "I forgot. There's a Rule Number Two. Do NOT, under any circumstance, close the—

A metal *clink* was heard, as if the hinged lid on the Shining Trapezohedron's box had been snapped closed.

"—lid!"

But it was already too late for that. There was an infernally loud *boom,* almost as if a bomb had fallen on the church, and then a series of moderate tremors embraced the structure, shaking dust and bits of plaster from the top of the spiral stairs.

Everard yelled, "Lillibridge! Get out of there!" but the only responses that the newspaperman could muster were screams.

A rapid series of *thunks* was also apparent, as though Lillibridge were being tossed back and forth ragdoll-style and slammed against the walls. Everard leapt up two steps, feeling he should go into the room and help Lillibridge but—

More screams made him lose his nerve. What could he do anyway? He already knew the outcome of the violent event, and Asenath had said so herself, *Otherwise, there'll be TWO melted skeletons that Blake finds.*

Poor Lillibridge...

Through one of the lancet windows in the side of the stairwell, the sunlight returned as the clouds had moved off.

The next sound he heard was something like a

grunt—but not a *human* one—like some beast subjected to a sudden anguish, and then he heard a loud *SLAM!*

He stood there for full minutes, listening, but heard nothing now.

In and out, real quick, he told himself. With sunlight in the room, he knew that the *thing* would be quelled for the time being, and just in case, he turned on the cellphone's flashlight app. Then he rushed back into the room.

The sizzling sound he heard was nauseating; he knew what it was. There was the sunlight shining through the louvers, and there was the golden storage box for the Shining Trapezohedron, its lid still closed by Lillibridge's unknowing hand.

As quickly as he could, Everard flipped the lid back open. He noticed that the red striations threaded along the stone's black bulk seemed to be throbbing, and when he touched it—"Shit!"—he snapped his hand away because the oval stone's surface was so hot now that it left actual burns on his fingers.

When he looked up at the trapdoor in the ceiling, he knew what had happened. *Lillibridge unknowingly closed the lid at the same time the clouds drifted across the sun. Suddenly the chamber was just dark enough to summon the thing up in the steeple room. It came down, did the job on Lillibridge, but then retreated back up there when the clouds moved off and brightened the room again.*

He took one look past the pedestal the stone sat on, looked down, and saw what was left of Lillibridge. The man was still sizzling, cooking. His ribs had been pulled open and were curled unnaturally outward. His abdominal cavity had been emptied, and so had his cranial vault because Everard could see that too, through the circular hole that the entity —the Haunter—had made. *Fuck this,* he thought, gagging. He rushed out of the room, followed by the sizzling and an aroma like roasted pork, and he closed the door.

What a pile of shit day this turned out to be, he thought. He trudged down the spiral staircase. Puffs of decade-old dust rose up and he walked quickly along a row of doors hidden by apsidal arches that paralleled the western pews. Then he barged past the first door that read VESTRY. A scroll-top desk stood open, and there was an old shoe box filled with a variety of cellphones. The ones that had retained the most battery power he loaded into his pockets. The darkening red light in the stained-glass windows told him that dusk would soon be upon him. *What's gonna happen then?* Came the dreadful question. *Is that thing in the attic gonna come down here and barbeque me?* In the story, the outside streetlights were sufficient to keep the thing in the church, but...

What do I know? What if it's a darker than average night? What if clouds cover the moon and stars just like they'd blocked out the sun earlier?

He shoved the grim speculations away and tried to keep focused. Here was a closet filled, indeed, with the clerical vestments of the Church of Starry Wisdom: orange and red cloaks, and similar miters but with piping of the same off-gold that the Shining

Trapezohedron's box was made of. Nothing else of interest could be found in the closet, so he nosed around the other side of the room. Here, the stained-glass windows seemed more vibrant, as if the growing darkness outside increased the clarity of the light in the windows, and these were the grimmest renderings yet. A man strung up by his ankles was visible only from the waist to the feet because everything from the waist to head had been submerged into a cauldron of either boiling water or boiling oil. Women in the next window's background were being sexually mauled by creatures that seemed half-human and half-toad; in the foreground orange-and-red cloaked ministers appeared to be crushing the heads of more naked women—some quite pregnant—with sledgehammers. The last window Everard allowed himself to look at showed a pile of human babies being buried in hot coals by still more shovel-bearing members of the Church of Starry Wisdom.

Make me puke! He thought. He staggered back and could only pray that the depictions in the windows were not based on actual events...

He noticed some smaller drawers in the scroll-top, so he rifled through them, pleased to discover a small five-shot revolver that said on its side Remington-Beals Model 1-.31. It was loaded so he stuffed it in his pocket. Everard was against all private handgun ownership... until now. *Can't hurt to have it,* he thought. Next he found some yellowed envelopes, some ink wells and pens, and a roll of stamps from the day. Then...

In one slot was simply a piece of parchment paper

rolled up into a tube. Everard flattened it out on the desk and stared at it with intense curiosity. Florid handwriting looked back at him like a mocking enigma:

Centagon: 100-sided polyhedron - IN
Enneahedron: 9-sided polyhedron - WH
Decagon: 10-sided polyhedron - DW

Hexakosihexekontahexagon: 666-sided polyhedron - Back

More fucked up stuff... Everard was no geometry afficionado, but this list clearly named more stones akin to the Shining Trapezohedron. But what purpose did they serve? Were they like the Shining Trapezohedron in that they summoned entities from the Otherworld? Did they show other dimensions if stared at?

And those letters at the end of each line? He wondered. *What do they mean? And then, at the end of the last line, the word "back?"*

Everard shrugged. *Guess I'll just have to find a hexakosihexekontahexagon to find out, for FUCK'S sake!*

He put the paper in his pocket and continued snooping around. Another drawer revealed—

What have we here?

He pulled out an envelope with the address PROVIDENCE TELEGRAM, 619 Comstock Rd. In the upper right corner was a two-cent stamp displaying a rifled minuteman, and a post mark that read 1851. Scribbled in the upper left was the name J. Lanagan and an East Providence address.

Lanagan, he tossed the name around in his mind. *Lanagan...* Of course, in "Haunter of the Dark" Lillibridge referred to a photographer named Lanagan who'd evidently taken a picture of the church in 1851. Someone in the congregation must've pilfered this envelope somehow, perhaps a postal employee.

Everard opened the envelope and whisked out a stack of four-by-three photos. They weren't daguerreotypes but instead the more popular paper-backed calotypes. The very first photo showed the church in a much grander state than it was now: no grime-smudged outer brick walls, no broken windows, no fallen minarets or crumbled buttresses. Someone had written on the back: Starry Wisdom, 1851. More photos followed this: interior pictures and various parishioners: women in bonnets and bustles dresses, and men in the then-stylish long-tailed jackets and high collars. The next photos were shot from a longer distance in, of all places, the woods, as if Lanagan were trying hard to take the photos without being seen. Cloaked and hooded members of the Church of Starry Wisdom were busying themselves around some sort of stone altar. One member was stropping a long knife, another was starting a fire under an elevated iron cage; Everard couldn't tell from the smoke, and he hoped his eyes were deceiving him, but there seemed to be a shape—a *human* shape—packed into the cage.

Then came the last photo, which caused Everard to faint and clunk to the floor.

In this one another cloaked and hooded figure seemed to be tending to several bubbling cauldrons, and the altar now had several objects set on it: more polyhedron gems, the smallest the size of a lemon, the largest the size of a warped basketball. There must've been a dozen of them there, and they all sat in asymmetrical bright metal boxes similar to that of the Shining Trapezohedron.

But the figure was looking up, right at the camera. Smiling.

It was Asenath, and all around her, the world went black.

6

When he awoke, it was significantly darker. A single feeble stream of moonlight skimmed over the top of the wood boarding up the broken window to his right, falling on the mangy carpet upon which he had collapsed.

Where was he? For several moments, he couldn't quite remember. His head felt heavy, as if stuffed so full of cotton that it muted his senses. He blinked as his eyes adjusted to the gloom around him.

Then, with sudden, stomach-turning clarity, it all came back to him—the church, the Shining Trapezo-hedron, poor Lillibridge... and Asenath. He was alone, drugged, and certainly far from any sense of home or safety, and if the fiction of someone Everard was coming to believe to be a mad god were true, then he was good and screwed.

He was still in the church... the one Lovecraft

himself had described as "the seat of an evil older than mankind and wider than the known universe."

He caught his breath, listening for the thing—the Haunter—moving around upstairs, but heard nothing. He had to think, *think!* What had happened in the story after Lillibridge was killed? The body would be discovered and would raise questions. There would be rumors, wild theories, many of which were closer to the mark than the theorists would ever know... and then a physician, possibly Lillibridge's examining physician, would throw the stone in the bay, thinking he had destroyed it and spared the earth a monstrosity which never should have been here in the first place. It wouldn't keep, though—not if Robert Blake's mysterious death forty-two years later was any indication.

But none of that had happened yet... had it? How did time work here? And better yet—where was "here," *really*?

He tried to stand and immediately regretted it as a wave of nausea washed down from what seemed like the crown of his head to the lower depths of his gut. He reeled against the desk, eyes closed, and after a minute or so, the sensation passed. Whatever Asenath had given him, it sure was strong, and clearly wasn't out of his system yet.

He pushed away the nagging doubt that it ever would be.

"I've got to get out of here," he muttered to the empty room, and then found himself cringing at the thought that somebody or some*thing* might actually answer him.

No one did. *Thank the universe for life's small blessings*, he thought sarcastically.

He collected himself and stood upright. Whatever else was going on, he couldn't let anyone find him in the church with the body—not the authorities or the good old superstitious townsfolk, not the Starry Wisdom cultists... and not the Haunter.

He glanced at the door to the office and frowned. He couldn't remember if he'd shut it himself when he'd first come in here, but that seemed a secondary concern, given what was tacked to the door itself, just about eye level.

It was a photograph not unlike those he'd found in the Lanagan envelope: a four by three black and white shot of... a sign?

He lurched toward the door and squinted at the picture. It was a photo of a signpost, angled upward as if taken from the street. The sign itself was little more than a crude wooden board nailed to the post at the top. Its contents appeared to be carved thinly into the wood by maybe a pocketknife or something. He read the words and the frown deepened.

LOOK BEHIND YOU, ASSHOLE

He felt a chill that rippled across the back of his neck, making him shiver. It was stupid, really, the idea that a picture of a sign from some point in the past could have anything to do with him, *him specifically*, in the here and now, and yet...

He didn't want to look.

Everard could feel something, though, in that

same vague but sure way a person can sense eyes boring into his back or his face or feel the substantive bulk someone takes up, even as unseen, unheard space.

He *really* didn't want to look.

With a short intake of breath, Everard whirled around.

There, on the floor where he had come to, sat a metal box with a golden hue that wasn't gold. The lid of the box was thrown back. The interior lining was of a black so dark that it conjured images of deep space, of space between realities, within the void, but it was far from the most impressive or terrifying of the box's contents. That particular honor went to the multi-faceted stone hanging suspended above the black from multiple brass tines, a stone even blacker than the interior itself, with pulsing bright blue veins threaded across its surfaces.

The stone was large, at least a foot or two in circumference, Everard guessed, and had more facets than he could count. It looked almost like a disco ball from hell. If he had to venture a guess (and he supposed, given his current situation, he did), it might have been a hundred different sides, maybe more.

What had the list said?

Centagon: 100-sided polyhedron – IN

That sounded about right. He crept cautiously toward it, careful not to look into the stone. As he got closer, he felt a chill, and as he crouched near the thing, he shivered. He couldn't stop himself from reaching out and touching one of the surfaces with the tip of his finger and was surprised and a little repulsed by how cool it was to the touch, and... clammy. Like wet skin—cold wet skin.

Cold wet dead skin.

Stop.

He drew his hand away. Could *IN* mean... a way in? Into his own world, his own reality? He glanced around, saw the parchment with the polyhedron notations curled up on the floor nearby, and swiped it, rolling it tightly and tucking it into his back pocket. It might be useful later, he supposed. He thought of taking the photo of Asenath with the stones, too, but he couldn't quite bring himself to look for it, let alone touch it.

Instead, he turned back to the stone in the metal box before him. His knees were starting to ache, crouched on the floor like that, but he ignored their groaning.

Would he have to look into it? Or maybe—

Before he could decide what to do next, the lid flew closed. Dizziness enveloped him again; and his vision began to disintegrate into black spots.

"No! No no no..." He thought he heard the low tone of a bell—from the steeple?—and the cry of the Haunter or maybe a gull, and then all went black again.

7

In the dark in-between place, Everard saw a thousand hells, and in them, millions of cruelties—countless scenarios where tragedy, indignity, and despair might have been an actual respite from the horror, where the capacity for ugliness and unbound evil was limitless. It might have driven him insane if it had lasted longer than a single moment, if he had been left to linger for any length of time in that place where incongruous geometries spilled one world into another, but he hadn't. He emerged elsewhere, with the fleeting ephemera of dread like an echo, and Everard's mind—at least the conscious part of it—didn't retain any of it.

In fact, the first thing Everard was aware of as he came to again was the wash of cold over his legs, and a dull, rhythmic roaring in his ears.

He opened his eyes. Above him was an overcast sky, heavy with the threat of rain and the smell of fish. Beneath him, the ground was grainy. His legs felt wet.

Everard sat up.

He found himself on a beach, with the waves of low tide washing against his feet and the cuffs of his pants. Behind him, tall grasses whispered and shivered in the dull breeze. In front of him, the dark gray ocean made sullen passes at the shoreline.

About a quarter of a mile down the beach seemed to be some sort of fishing village. Everard could see a bit of it just inland—mostly crumbling houses with decaying gambrel roofs and gables huddled together. A few had steeples whose tops had caved in, and a couple yawned with black, empty holes. Most of the roofs of the houses he could see had caved in completely.

Everard saw a few large square Georgian houses with cupolas and railed widow's walks further inland. They looked a little less like kindling waiting to catch fire, he supposed. From his vantage point, though, much of the town, what was left of it, was falling apart, and whatever else it offered further from the shore was obscured, including any residents.

Most of the view down the beach was of the dilapidated waterfront. Its sand-choked harbor was enclosed by an old stone breakwater, within which, on a relatively small bump of sand, sat decrepit cabins, moored dories, and scattered lobster pots. The wharves extended into the water at different lengths, depending on how far decay had swallowed their ends. The stone foundations of what might once have been a lighthouse were perched a little higher; there, Everard thought he saw movement, but couldn't make out the details of those people, probably fishermen, who were moving. A small building with a white belfry gave off a sense of the industrial like it might be a factory, but no one seemed to be moving anything in or out. The sea and the river seemed to meet there, washing past a mix of the old and the older still, of structures passively standing and the actively falling apart.

The stench of fish was overpowering, so much so that Everard began to look for the source. There was none immediately visible, at least on the beach. He glanced out into the water and saw a black line of rock about a mile and a half out.

And he recognized it—and by degrees, the decomposing town that faced it—but not from any place he'd ever actually been. Devil Reef did look, though, as he'd always imagined it.

"Fuck me," Everard muttered. "This is bad."

Innsmouth. He was in Innsmouth.

He stood on shaky legs and gazed at the water uneasily. Salty spray pattered his face, and the cool breeze dried it almost immediately to a stickiness on his skin. Normally, Everard loved the beach—the sand, the surf, the sun, the young girls in bikinis, all of it—but this... something felt very wrong about all of this: the sun and its meager light forever darting behind clouds, the insistent way the grains of sand and salt, carried by water stricken a murky blue-gray, sprayed and ground against him, and the noisome breeze that dried it all like a filmy second skin on his face and arms... he didn't like it, not at all.

The wind shifted direction and hit him full in the face with the unwholesome smell of things rotting on the beach, and probably not all of them fish...

In the distance, a low bell tolled, and he found himself heading toward the sound before he was even fully aware that he was doing it.

"This is going to go badly," he muttered to the surf. A monstrous thing in a church steeple was problem enough; a whole town of misshapen, squamous things flopping, sliding, and slithering after him, intent on killing him or feeding him to some fish god or forcing him to fuck some deep-ocean she-beast... he shivered.

Credit where credit's due, motherfucker, he thought. *Kudos to HPL for some really horrifying shit in one of his stories, at least.*

He turned away from the beach and onto a road as soon as he saw one. He didn't relish wandering around town, but some inner part of him couldn't bear to be near the water anymore. *Not that the smell in the town proper is any better,* he thought.

Among the crumbling buildings, sagging on their decaying foundations, he saw no one, but he felt watched. Shutters in upstairs windows closed before he could catch a glimpse of the inhabitants behind them. At every corner, someone—something—turned and moved out of sight just before he could see them. Clothes hung from laundry lines, threadbare, stretched out, and still somehow dirty, and children's toys—a ball, jacks, an odd ugly dolly—

appeared on sidewalks or sparse scrub grass patches that he supposed served as lawns. Someone had to be living there, he supposed—he knew, of course; he'd read the story—but they were staying well out of sight.

As he shuffled along, he stepped on something both rigid and squishy, and he flinched, thinking, *It's a hand, a hand, oh GOD, I've stepped on a—*

He looked down and saw it was a large man's shoe, its sole peeling away. Both the arch and heel were distended, as if some other kind of foot had tried to force it on... or had worn it until its transformation made the shoe an impossible fit.

Everard shook his head. He didn't like the kinds of thoughts that this place worked into his head, the way the salt and sand had worked into his skin. Those thoughts felt filmy, itching and grinding against the soft parts of his brain.

His feet (he was pretty sure it wasn't his brain making decisions just then) led him uphill over grassy bluffs and windswept outcroppings until he turned onto a large semicircular stone square on which sat a tall, cupola-crowned building with remnants of yellow paint.

Above the door was a sign, although the paint and, to some extent the wood itself, had worn away most of the lettering. Still, Everard knew the place.

He had found the Gilman House Hotel.

8

Everard was about to enter the seedy, multi-storied hotel but then thought better of it after remembering Lovecraft's *Shadow Over Innsmouth,* and what happened to the protagonist after booking a room there. *Fuck this,* he thought and strode off in the opposite direction. Dusk was already lowering itself upon the town and windows came alight in some of the ramshackle dwellings. Shadows filled the streets that he could see and among them, it seemed, people were emerging, just groups of two or three, some limping or oddly stooping as they walked. Everard found it impossible to push the story out of his head; he knew who or what these people were. After straying a ways from the hotel, he found a bench flanked by some browning bushes; he sat down to contemplate his next move.

Okay, let me sort all this crazy shit out in my mind. Back at the Church of Starry Wisdom, after Lillibridge got burnt to a crisp, I went downstairs and found that other polyhedron in one of the vestry rooms. It must've been the Centagon mentioned on the parchment list because when I looked in it—a perfect black stone with illumined blue striations—my consciousness fizzed out and then I found myself here, in a carbon copy of Lovecraft's hive of monsters known as Innsmouth. What can I do now?

Something in his common sense, if he had any left, suggested that the secret to traversing this Other World must involve other stones, as the parchment list implied. He'd already found the Shining Trapezohedron and now the Centagon. Therefore, further transport must rely on his finding the other stones on the list. One of them *must* be the means with which he could exit this nightmare and get back to where he'd come from: the convention back at the Double Tree Hotel in Williamsburg.

So, where's the next stone? He wondered, awash in aggravation. He looked up abruptly at the rising sound of an automobile engine and noticed a rattletrap bus pull up in front of the Gilman House. *The bus from the story,* he recalled. *Joe Sargent's bus, delivers the story's protagonist to the town.* Everard watched with interest. A tall stoop-shouldered man with immense hands and feet stepped off the bus; he was wearing some sort of blue uniform and a gray golfer's-type cap; he trudged toward the hotel entrance but then curiously stopped, stood still a moment, and then—

Oh, shit...

—he stared straight at Everard. Everard gulped.

Even at this distance, Everard could discern the physical details made famous in Lovecraft's story: the

"Innsmouth look." The man seemed only part-human, with an odd narrow head and overlarge circular eyes, akin to goggles, which were bright blue, watery, and unblinking. He had a small, large-lipped mouth, almost—

Almost like a fish...

Joe Sargent stared back for an uncomfortably long time, but someone else had exited the bus as well, a slender, normal-looking young man in a cheap suit and tie, and he carried with him a valise.

That's got to be him, Everard knew. *Olmstead, the main character...* In the printed story, this protagonist was never named, but in a discarded draft, the character's name was given as Robert Olmstead, a young man treating himself to a sightseeing tour along the New England coast, mainly in search of unique architecture.

What to do? Everard mused. His first inclination was to rush over there and warn Olmstead what lay in store for him, but then he forbore the urge when he remembered that Olmstead would survive the monstrous onslaught of the story. Warning him might throw some Mandela-Effect monkey wrench into the fabric of things, which might conceivably get Olmstead killed. *No. leave it be...*

Next, he put two and two together and reasoned this: he'd come upon the first two polyhedrons in a church—the Church of Starry Wisdom. Therefore, the logical place to search for the next stone might easily be a church as well. And he knew which church...

The Esoteric Order of Dagon.

The same church in whose doorway Olmstead

had seen a sinister priest in orange and red raiment, wearing a warped tiara atop his head. And where was this church?

One of several in the New Church Green...

"Ye be not from these parts, eh?" a sudden crackly old voice surprised him. "I kin tell ye ain't tetched like most folk heer."

Everard looked up quickly to see a bent, very old man standing before him. Frail, long white beard, and clothes that seemed composed of patched-together squares of sundry fabric. And the ancient man carried with him a most challenging odor that nearly racked Everard in his seat on the bench. At a glance, he knew who this man was.

Zadok Allen, the nonagenarian born and raised here in Innsmouth. He could be likened to the town wise man or, perhaps more accurately, the town drunk.

"No, I'm not from these parts," Everard confirmed. Whenever the breeze changed, he had to hold his breath against the stultifying b.o. "Just passing through."

"Look like thet devil Joe Sargent got his fishy eyes on ya. Take keer araound that one. Hear me well."

"Yes, Joe Sargent. He does seem to have taken note of me. I can't imagine why."

"Cain't ye?"

Everard noticed that Sargent, even now, was still staring at him, and also, too, at Zadok Allen.

"Give me the shivers, thet one, just as most of 'em do. Part'a the Marsh bloodline on the fust wife's side. En't nothin' right abaout the lot've 'em."

And this old guy would know, Everard realized. *He'd lived through the rise and fall of the Marsh Refining Company, and the invasion of the entire town at the hands of the Deep Ones, the sheer slaughter of hundreds of townsfolk, which included Allen's own father. He'd watched that slaughter as a child, poor bastard...*

"Might ye have a few pennies, sir?" Zadok Allen finally got to his own point, "to help this oldster fetch hisself a wee libation?"

Everard opened his wallet to search for an older-looking bill. He pulled out a crumbled one, hoping that it didn't look all too different from what was issued in the late '20s. "I hope this helps—"

Zadok snatched the bill up with a gleam in his eyes of someone decades younger. "What a fine sir ye be ta so help out an old stick like myself! Thank ye kindly!"

"You're welcome," Everard said. "But now maybe you can help me. I'm anxious to find the New Church Green—"

Zadok Allen seemed to turn into a terrified scarecrow at this information. "No. Ya ain't! Satan's Circle's what we few decent folks call thet infernal place! That blasted church droved all the real churches out'a taown and the passons with 'em. And some'a them passons *disserpeered!* Found one of 'em chopped up'n pieces down near the waterfall by the old Rawley line. Probably Father Dunning, they think, of the New Congregational Church. He mouthed off against the Marshes one time too much and... he weren't seen more."

Now, here was some new information, for sure.

And this was Zadok's way of telling Everard the same could befall him. "Oh, I only wanted to see the area, that's all, for the architecture," he sluffed.

"Best ya steer clear. Strange noises come aout'a there at night, screamin' like, bellowin' and sech. You should heer them things a-howlin' and a-barkin' and a-floppin' abaout. Nay, ye daon't wanna *know* what all goes on..."

Don't worry, I already do. "Oh I have no intention to go inside, just wanted to walk by."

"Wall, all rights, I s'pose there ain't no harm, long as ye mind what I say." The old man's withered finger pointed down the street. "Follow this road daown theer, walk a couple'a minutes, and there be the Green..."

Everard nodded thanks and old Zadok Allen rushed off in the opposite direction as the streets grew darker and darker. *I guess I could use a stiff drink myself...*

His convention shoes, the black dressy ones from Men's Warehouse, clapped down the cracked side-walk, and with each step, the coming dusk seemed to darken. From afar, he finally noticed more groups of pedestrians clumped together as if wary of their surroundings. Everard noticed one shapely young woman with long shiny blond hair and a very comely bosom. She was holding hands with a limping man beside and when she turned to take note of Everard—

Holy shit!

—the woman's face seemed to be pressed to one side of her head, two eyes on the left side and none on the right, like—

Like a flounder...

He didn't dare think of what her genitals were like at this stage of transformation. And just then, at the sound of a wet, slopping-like heavy breathing, a squat man with a great lumpen belly hobbled down the other side of the road, carrying an overlarge sack of clams or oysters over his shoulders. Big watery eyes appraised Everard, and the man seemed to nod a haphazard greeting. Chilled, Everard nodded back but blanched when he noticed the man's angled face and lack of anything like a nose. His ears more resembled fins on the side of his head, but perhaps that was just the power of suggestion working on Everard's already tainted imagination.

The infrequent streetlamps sputtered every few blocks. He couldn't tell if they were incandescent or the old "town-gas" elements that burned gasified coal; he could hear them hissing. Beyond ranks of high bushes, he could glimpse more stately abodes in fair repair, with high narrow windows and square Georgian roofs. Did he hear a faint *thumping* coming from one such attic, and a wet, sloppy cough or yelp?

Everard shuddered.

Finally, an old, faded sign announced NEW CHURCH GREEN as the road opened into a wide circle. But any "green" that might have existed here in the past had long gone over to browned scrub grass and spindly twigs for trees.

Up in the murky, darkening sky, Everard noticed multiple church steeples standing at varying distances, several with holes for where clockfaces should be, several more with belfries that housed no bells. But here, at a closer church, a steeple pointed upward through sea mists, displaying a clockface with no hour or minute-hand, and odd configurations circumscribing the face. Were they astrological symbols? Closer now he saw that the body of the church seemed half-submerged into the ground; in other words, such that the nave and pews were reached by descending a short flight of steps, and the windows were more akin to basement windows at knee-level were one standing on the ground outside. Each window was a long, narrow rectangle, and most seemed filled with vaguely moving tendrils of orangish light. Also, almost inaudibly, Everard heard or *thought* he heard very low, suboctave bass notes as of a pipe organ.

Well, here it is, Everard thought. *How do I get in?*

Then he heard a *thunk* from behind the church and noticed a stooped-over man dragging some garbage cans outside; there were quite a few cans. Everard peered closer. The man, next, took the first can and dragged it farther behind the building, such that he seemed to disappear. The sound of the metal can scraping old asphalt was more than apparent. That's when Everard took a few more steps and craned his neck around the back of the church. Not far off stood an incinerator whose chimney liberally gushed. The stooped attendant threw open an iron hatch then began to heave parcels of garbage into the fire.

Now's my chance, Everard reasoned, and with a tenor of bravado not common to him, he skirted around the closer trash cans in search of the back door to the church. But one errant glance down into one of the cans caused him to lurch and nearly vomit.

In the flickering light, his eyes detected, first, body parts—*human* body parts—laying amid the garbage as if tossed there: severed hands and feet, forearms, thighs, and the like. They seemed to be the limbs of young adults; in fact, one such severed head was that of dead-eyed blond girl not even out of her teens. *Fuck me!* Everard thought. He knew the wisest thing to do was run, but something—some imp of the perverse in his psyche—prevented such a flight, leaving him helpless to stare down into the next can.

No, no, no...

Everard staggered blind away from the can, gagging and feeling for the back door. Sweat poured down his face. There could be no mistake as to what he saw: a pile of at least a dozen severed baby heads...

He nearly lost his footing upon entering the church through the rear door. *My God, what am I doing here?* A nearly lightless corridor led away toward some sort of ingress tinged with more faint orange light. He knew it was crazy for him to enter this church, but he also knew there was no other choice. The entire *scenario* was crazy; it was impossible, yet here he was, standing in the middle of the impossibility. *Just look for the polyhedron,* words from nowhere seemed to pound into his head. But there was no telling it would even be here. What must he do then? Search the whole town?

He crept around a corner into a brighter wedge of light and glimpsed the long flank of empty pews. Just beside him stood a worm-eaten bookshelf which boasted a Greek *Necronomicon* and an Old German copy of *De Vermis Mysteriis*. *Goddamn, this shit's all real...* But he didn't want to see what other forbidden tomes lurked on the shelf. Up past the nave and towards the altar, two figures in orange and red gowns passed a clear goblet back and forth, each taking sips. Obviously a most unholy communion: the goblet was full of what could only be blood. *The priests,* Everard knew, *the ministers of the Esoteric Order of Dagon...* Just like in the story, the pair of wardens had oddly asymmetrical tiaras atop their heads, the tiaras forged of something even more resplendent than gold and fitted with glittering gemstones whose color defied sane description. Over the altar was draped a diaphanous black cloth with silver fringe, and upon this was embroidered a series of cryptic hieroglyphs and ghastly depictions of vaguely tentacled monsters bearing only the most outre approximations to human physicality. The heads of the beings were nauseating even to blink at, like great inflamed carbuncles centered by gaping orifices that might be sockets for massive gelatinous eyes. Everard nearly moaned aloud: *Why the FUCK did I ever go to that damn convention?*

But more nauseating even than the effigies on the altar-cloth were those deep but barely aural organ notes that seemed to throb paradimensionally about the orange-tinged space of the church interior. This music was not J.S. Bach, but something so deviously composed as to upheave one's very soul: deep subterranean notes of incogitable discord and cacodemoniacal mindlessness. It was disorienting him, fogging his brain. From his niche, he tried to look more solidly at the two priests, but then he noticed a sconce of some sort just *behind* the altar, and in it sat—

I don't believe it! I found it immediately!

The sconce housed another polyhedron, something more square than rounded, rather squashed as it glittered from its opened box. About two feet long and one and a half high, and its color seemed to be a murky blend of violet, heather-green, and maroon. This one, like the others, possessed thread-thin striations that seemed to luminesce but in a blinding white, like burning magnesium. It didn't seem to have many facets at all, so it surely wasn't the 666-sided hexakosihexekontahexagon listed on the parchment. Whichever it was, it didn't matter. *I HAVE to get to that stone...*

Just as he was about to lurch forward toward the priests, a hand slapped across his face from behind. It was a huge fishy-smelling hand, bigger than the circumference of a dinner plate, and when the fat, calloused fingers depressed, Everard yelled out at the pain; it was as though his face were being compressed in a vice. Behind him, he could feel his attacker's other hand yanking down Everard's pants...

Holy FUCK!

He strained his neck to catch a sliver of a glance at the face of his attacker and then nearly passed out when he recognized noseless bulge-eyed bus driver Joe Sargent who chuckled now, gurglingly, as that same preposterously large hand marauded Everard's shrinking genitals.

"E-yuh," Sargent guttered, "This puny stuff?

I'se'll scrape it right off'a ye with my fish-gutter'n make a woman of ya. Then I'll suck alls the blood aout, and give it ta Azathoth..."

Perhaps worse than this gargling threat was how Everard could now feel Sargent lowering his own trousers behind him, the action of which released something—an erection, no doubt—that had to be the size of a ten-pound haddock. "But fust, I'll'se help meself to a piece'a this citified ass... Git it right up in thar. Deep."

Everard was effortlessly shoved down to the floor on his belly, his legs splayed, and then positioned to affect rape. Until then, the only thing to ever be stuck in Everard's anus was a doctor's finger, but if Sargent managed to slide in that monstrosity of a cock, Everard couldn't possibly survive the resultant hemorrhage of blood.

Sargent's free hand smashed Everard's face against the floor, and he could feel a slimy glans working its way against his sphincter.

"Ee-yuh. Jess ye wait till I'se git it stuffed all the way up ye..."

Everard had no intention of waiting for anything of the sort. Some component of his survival instinct continued working, and without much conscious thought, he'd dug the pistol out of his bunched up pants pocket and—

BAM!

—managed to squeeze off a round backward and over his shoulder. He heard a loud barrel-chested "UGH," and then felt the colossal weight roll off his body. When he managed to churn himself upright, there lay Joe Sargent, minus the top half of his warped skull, phlegm-like loops of brains slopped across the floor, and his appallingly large cock twitching in death throes.

Fuck him, Everard thought, and then quickly knelt upright with his pants still bunched at his knees, and—

BAM!

—hit the first bellowing priest right between the ichthyic eyes. The tiara blew off his warped head first, followed by everything else from the eyes up, mostly oatmeal-like mush the color of peas.

The second priest, even more outraged than the first, plodded forward, rowing arms as long as an orangutan's. Everard felt calm in spite of this. First he drew a bead on the priest's pointed forehead but stalled and thought, *No, no, this guy goes out in style,* then lowered the sites, let out a breath, and—

BAM!

"Yes, sir! Got'cha right in the fish-dick!"

The priest released a heavy bubbling vocal protestation while clutching his blood-pumping crotch. He convulsed as one being electrocuted.

Not bad, Everard congratulated himself, *for a guy who's never fired a gun before.*

He wasted no more time and jogged up behind the altar to address with his eyes the large violet-green-maroon polyhedron in its gleaming, opened box. The odd shape, like a cube that had been pressed out of its contours, showed no signs of scores of minuscule facets. Instead there were only a handful of warped rectangular facets which made Everard think of large fishnet stockings. When he managed to accurately count them he discovered there were only nine such facets.

This had to be the *Enneahedron:* the nine-sided polyhedron inscribed on the parchment, with the two-letter suffix WH.

What the hell is WH?

But there was little time to contemplate; he had to get out of here. He placed a hand on each end of the large stone and could feel its heat beating at once. Was it actually minutely increasing and decreasing in size? He focused on the near-blinding-white striations which also seemed to throb like arteries connected to a heart. And the odd mix of hues between the striations seemed to dissolve in and out of each other. All he could think to do was repeat his previous tactic and violate the implicit rule from the story: he stared directly into the stone...

His consciousness felt like something solid straining to transform to liquid. Was there something in the stone *sucking* on the myriad electrical activity of his brain? More white-hot striations seemed to stretch weblike across the purlieu of his visuality. His mind seemed to *bend;* it *stretched* as if his skull had dissolved, leaving only his raw brain which was siphoned through his eyeholes and somehow sucked into the deepening tunnel of what he was seeing. Now his eyeless vision was forced to gaze amid a distant sound like maniacal flutes.

Next he saw cities, or things like cities: a geometric demesne of impossible architecture that extended in a long vanishing line of horrid black—a raging *terra dementata.* Concaved horizons crammed with stars, or things like stars, sparkled close against cubist chasms. He saw buildings and streets, tunnels and tower blocks, strange, flattened factories whose chimneys gushed oily smoke. It was a necropolis, systematized and endless, bereft of error in its moving angles and lines. It was pandemonium...

And he saw people too. Or things *like* people.

One of the things was waving at him, beckoning him. Where its head should be sprouted a fat tentacle with tiny pins in the circles of its suckers...

Then a sound, louder than anything he'd ever conceived, exploded around his senses. He could only equate it to what he might expect a nuclear detonation to sound like, the insane sonic wave behind a power sufficient enough to destroy whole cities in an irreducible fraction of a second...

But next, the star-lit black sky over the ghastly necropolis seemed to tear, as fabric might, forming a vertical clough which shimmered in colors wholly alien to any sane spectrum. Like a telescope with a zoom lens, Everard's disembodied vision shot into the midst of that clough and left him adrift to suddenly find his capacity for vision gazing at never-ending mountain ranges, only the mountains were composed of immense crystals dozens of miles high. The peaks of such mountains poked through banks of luminous clouds that were either cerulean-blue or magenta-pink. The clouds throbbed and seemed to turn themselves inside-out at the places where the mountain peaks penetrated. Closer inspection showed Everard plateaus braced against the mountainsides, and from these plateaus rose prismoid structures of dark dazzling colors. Everard received the immediate impression that these structures were encampments of some sort or even cities, formed of masses of myriad geometric shapes, some blinking with pinpoints of non-chromatic lights and others lurking in some mode of physical darkness. Just as Everard felt the encapsulation of his awareness begin to drift one such pandemonic mass—

—the explosive sound shrank and seemed to shift into a loud *clank!* This snapped Everard's concentration off the stone; his heart was thundering. As he tried to shake off his grogginess, he looked in a panic toward the dark corridor which had led him here from outside and saw—

Damn it! I forgot about him!

Lumbering toward him now, sort of clodhopping like someone only partly ambulatory, came the custodian he'd seen outside, loading receptacles full of human body parts into the incinerator, and with him, into the nave, came a sickening aroma of hot ashes and roasted pork.

The thing barreled toward him, arms rowing, huge circular eyes raving hatred. It grunted meaningless noises like, "E uh glud shub nleb!" The custodian or man or thing was tramping forward, closing in fast—

An irregular instinct circumvented Everard's better judgment; instead of going for the pistol, he returned his attention to the polyhedron, lifted it up, and went back to staring directly into its shifting striations and unreckonable colors.

The howling custodian was now brandishing a long stem of iron as might be used to stir ashes; he raised it high, howled again, and swung the iron with all his or its might toward Everard's head—

swoosh—

The impossible panorama that was hijacking Everard's gaze somehow sucked his awareness back into the oscillating stone just as his attacker's weapon passed through the area of space that had, one second previously, been occupied by Everard's skull.

Everard disappeared into a screaming, raging, multicolored infinity—

The church, the monstrous custodian, and even the Enneahedron stone itself were gone, leaving him adrift back in the same maniacal geometric demesne he'd just a moment ago exploded out of. Now he floated closer to the structured masses of prisms, cubes, and polygonal shapes. Of a physical body he could only surmise that he no longer had one; instead he felt as though he was solely a mass of gyrating molecules being adhered together by some incontemplatable centrifugal force, and whatever this new-found vessel of his awareness might be, he felt buoyant amid the tepid, endless space that formed this new anti-human universe. Some kind of riptide of air—if "air" actually existed here—was towing him through all this arcane open space, toward another cleft in the mountainside, and into the nearest valley jammed with more functional geometric constructs. He nearly lost consciousness staring amazedly at what existed now before him: on each plateau stood more crystalline shapes: pyramids of some jasper-like stone, only many times larger than any pyramid on earth. These massive edifices sat on their pointed tips, not on their bases, and beyond the stratas within them, he noticed sentient objects sliding back and forth, like flecks or pepper. Were these "flecks" the actual inhabitants of this domain? Conical frustums of amethyst seemed attached to artificially constructed planes along the crystalline mountain surface; truncated octahedrons sat studded on other crags, glimmering in an impossible taupe glow; cuboid rectangles of molten wisteria-pink formed colosseum-like arenas off of glassine cliffs; spinning spheres and half-spheres seemed nestled precariously on more crystal stems where trees would grow up the faces of earthly mountains; scarlet and cobalt-blue pinnacles and minarets could be seen at farther distances, like some byzantine outlands; and, strangest of all, were free-floating flat cylinders of bright-russet material bisected axel-like by white-hot rods down the middle, spinning, spinning. What were these paraworldly objects, revolving like tops? Did people exist in them, or... *were* there any real people in this cosmic mayhem? As Everard drifted higher, he became aware of a *popping* sensation, and with each pop, a smaller prismoid shape appeared before his vision, as if materializing out of thin air. And just as he was aware of these smaller shapes, they seemed, somehow, to be aware of him. Might these entities be the extra-dimensional carriers for other venturers such as himself, beings from other planes of existence or other terrestrial planets, sucked into this realm from their native places? Cocoons of awareness from other worlds? If so, were they here by their own efforts, or had they been absconded with by the keepers of this impossible and immense fortress? Everard felt something with the kinship to a chill when he stared into one such vessel, an irregular tetrahedron glimmering in shifting colors like ultramarine, neon gray, and a periwinkle off-blue. Beyond the entity's warping facets Everard could swear he noticed things like *eyes* staring back at him, appraising him, only the eyes weren't spheroid but more angled like roundish double-pointed pyramids. Everard gulped, though he had no organs to do so, and attempted to scream, but all that his mouthless body would emit was a stark, cold, vibrating silence.

Just in time, another force pulled him away and higher, up close to the peaks of the crystal mountains themselves, and through the gaseous cloud cover of demoniacal illumination. He was helpless, he knew, having no say where he was being locomoted to, but finally—

Good God, what is THAT?

What he swiftly converged upon was a pale-violent construction he could only describe as a sail on a great ship, only the sail's dimensions were nothing like square, but instead it seemed warped like so much else in this province or territory or whatever it might really be, and this "sail" was not by any means symmetrical: instead one edge was pulled in from the right, while the opposite edge seemed kicked out at the bottom and shrunk at the top, and within all that were several other polygonal shapes, all irregular and leaning either toward one another or away. The further Everard contemplated this, the faster his being seemed to catapult toward it, and the next thing he knew, he was rocketed *into* it until he felt the substance of his vessel crack and disintegrate, and suddenly, he was but flittering powder being siphoned through some manner of hole or orifice, and after that—

9

thunk!

—he was dropped back into his own terrestrial world, or some facsimile thereof, hitting a floor of old wooden planks. Normal earthly air came back into his lungs; he felt like something that had just been rescued from drowning but not in water, in... something else.

Someone from the floor below yelled up, "Hey, Walter! Are you all right?"

Walter? Everard thought dumbly. *Who the hell is—*
"Um, yes, I'm fine. Just tripped is all."

"Good. Don't let Drombowski hear all that racket; we don't want him on the warpath again..."

Everard was duped and confused. When he looked around, flat on his back, he saw that he'd landed in a stark oak-planked room, with an iron-railed bed and a ramshackle chair and a table that seemed to suffice for a desk, for on it was a heap of books and scribbled-on notepapers. Aching, he dragged himself up to a standing position, and shuffled to the desk. Some of the book titles read: QUANTUM MECHANICS, NON-PERTURBATIVE DYNAMISM, EINSTEINIAN-ROSEN BRIDGES & NON-ORIENTABLE WORMHOLES. *Cosmology,* thought Everard. *Parallel universes...* An errant glance at a bookshelf showed him another tome: THE SIZE OF THE UNIVERSE by Willem De Sitter, and that's when it all clicked in his head. The polyhedron he'd used to escape the Esoteric Order of Dagon had been a nine-sided gem—an Enneahedron—and next to that name on the parchment had been the letters WH. *So that's where I am now!* He realized, *I'm in Keziah Mason's old room in Lovecraft's Dreams in the Witch-House!*

Yes, there could be no mistake. Tin strips along the old baseboards reminded him that *Walter,* the protagonist in the story, implored the landlord, Drombowski, to seal up rat holes, for at times rats seemed to seethe in the ancient walls. The grim pile of a mansion was pre-Revolutionary, and in this very room, back in the late 1690s, an old crone named Keziah Mason had practiced spells and other components of witchcraft. But Keziah was no mere witch; it turned out she'd also been a trans-dimensional traveler using elements of physics, non-Euclidian geometry, and cosmological formulae hidden in the nooks and crannies of handed-down superstitious lore, all this to serve her otherworldly master in the effort to solicit the Devil, or something *worse* than the Devil. And she had an ever-present familiar—a *rat*—who assisted her in this noxious onus. Children disappeared from the poorest sections of town, babies were sacrificed on Walpurgis and All Hallows Eve, all this and even more hideous things to seek favor from the Blind Idiot God and other anti-deities that had existed since before time began. To the townsfolk, the rat was referred to as "Brown Jenkin," and was not actually a rat but a hellish hybrid with a human face, and tiny human hands and feet, and it could speak all languages...

Now that he'd collected his thoughts, Everard cemented the assurance that he was indeed in the old witch's room: what would be the north wall seemed pressed unnaturally into the room from the top while the bottom of the same wall was built at an *outward* angle; additionally, the ceiling was angled downward, and when Everard's vision summed up the whole he found that the geometric composure of these freakish angles presented a shocking duplicate of the canted angles of the great "sail" through which he was pushed and then expelled here. The gist of the old woman's metaphysical science asserted that curvatures and lines inscribed on the proper structures actually sufficed as "guidelines" of a sort, which pointed to specific cosmic orifices that would lead the practiced traveler to alien domains and dimensions just like the domain he'd recently been ejected from, a *geometric* domain whose cities were prisms and polygons and whose mountainsides existed as miles-high eminences of crystalline deposits. He shuddered to think of the sheer *age* of these deposits:

phenomena that had surely existed since time immemorial.

Exhausted, Everard sat slumped on Walter's rack-like iron-railed bed. Did the arcane angles of the north wall reveal the faintest violet luminosity? *It must be my imagination,* he deduced. *The power of suggestion remnant from the story's details...* On the peeling, yellowed wallpaper he noticed hand-rendered scribblings in charcoal, no doubt evidence of Walter's wee-hour brainstorming. Walter, though an isolated social misfit and reclusive egghead, must actually have possessed a knowledge of theoretical multi-dimension physics that matched or even excelled the genius of the old witch; Walter, indeed, was the first to understand such mathematical and quantum mechanics in nearly 250 years. Variations of the Reimann equation were scribbled across the walls, along with Agnesi Curves, and superimposed geometrics. *This* was what Walter focused his intellect on as the dread Walpurgis Night approached, and his efforts had obviously succeeded at least several times. Since Walter had used such devices to move from this world to that other, couldn't Everard harness some similar energy to leave this ancient eyrie and relocate himself back to that blasted hotel in Williamsburg where this nightmare had started?

He knew his work was cut out for him: he must find the next polyhedron on the parchment list. He had an idea that he must find them in order (why else would they have been *written* in that order?) He looked at the parchment again:

Centagon: 100-sided polyhedron – IN
Enneahedron: 9-sided polyhedron – WH
Decagon: 10-sided polyhedron – DW
Hexakosihexekontahexagon: 666 sided poly-
hedron – Back

IN I already know stands for Innsmouth, and WH is the Witch-House that I'm sitting in right now. And the next stone, the Decagon, can only mean Dunwich—gee, I can't wait to go there! His only inclination was to assume that after he found the Decagon and was conveyed to Dunwich, the birthplace of Wilbur Whateley, he would then have to find this insane 666-sided stone called the Hexakosihexekontahexagon. And he could only hope that the "back" on the parchment meant that *that* was the device by which he'd be able to go *back* where he'd started from.

But where to look? *What a pain in the ass. I can't believe that big-tit bitch is doing this to me...* The Decagon had to be hidden somewhere in this enormous ramshackle house. The attic seemed a logical place to start, but he knew from the story that the attic had been sealed long ago with mortise pegs; getting in it would require tools—*loud* tools—at least a hammer and crowbar, and he'd have to somehow get in there without the less-than-pleasant landlord, Drombowski, hearing the racket. He didn't want to go to jail in the 1930's.

Another possibility was the open spaces behind the walls that were angled in and out, and the down-sloping ceiling. And if he had no luck there? *I'll have to search every room in this giant fuckin' piece of shit house—*

The cellphone in his pocket rang, startling him that he almost shouted aloud. He didn't have to guess who it was...

"Hello, Asenath..."

"Where are you now, professor?" her sexy, lilting voice inquired. "The last known domicile of Keziah Mason?"

"Yeah. The house is even uglier than it is in the story."

"Well, let's hope that you managed to cross paths with Keziah. Maybe you can snag a piece of ass, huh? I mean, that's all women are to you, right? Pieces of ass?"

"Come on, that's a bit much. Isn't it?" *And I never got a piece of yours... bitch!*

"And a desperate old fool like you would probably go for it, too. Where you are now, Keziah's over 300 years old. Right up your alley."

Everard frowned. "Is there a reason you called? Or did you just want to chit-chat?"

"You may be an academician and a professor, but you're really not that smart—"

"Thanks."

Her voice lowered over the line. It seemed mocking. "Are you getting hard listening to my voice?'

"I think I can answer that question with an emphatic and very resolute *no.*"

A chuckle floated out of the phone. "Anyway, I thought I'd help you out a little. Give you a clue."

"Clue for what?"

"Where the next stone is."

Everard perked up. "I would be... much obliged."

Asenath's voice paused, as if for amusement, and then, in a sing-songy tone, said, "Merrily, merrily, merrily, merrily," and then hung up.

Everard's eyes bloomed when he put the phone away. *I guess I'm not as dumb as she thinks,* he suggested to himself, because he knew instantly and exactly what she meant. He slipped out of the room and cruised down the stuffy corridor. *I gotta get downstairs and out of this house,* he knew, and he had no idea what explanation he would offer for his presence if he encountered another tenant or, worse, the landlord. The stairs creaked interminably as he made his way down, and when he was almost at the bottom of the landing, he stopped short, spying an older longhaired man who was bald on top disappear into his first-floor room. The door read MAZUREWICZ. *The loom-fixer,* Everard remembered, *was an early victim of Keziah and her hideous mascot.*

He slipped out the nine-paneled front door, managing to close it silently. Before he embarked across the crabgrass-riddled front yard, something on the door grasped his eye: the doorknocker. It was a blank brass plate in the shape of a face but displaying only two eyes. For some reason it gave him the willies, so he took longer strides across the yard and behind the house. Asenath's allusion to the "Row, row, row the boat" song reminded him that, in the story, Walter had "rowed out twice to the ill-regarded island in the river, and made a sketch of the singular angles described by the moss-grown rows of gray standing stones..." *So I'll do the same thing,* Everard decided. *Doesn't sound too difficult unless, well, there's no fuckin' boat.* If so, he'd have to improvise, he supposed. But first he'd have to find the river, not any *real* river but the river made famous by Lovecraft's fiction: the Miskatonic River.

Outside was completely dark now, with no perceptible sounds from the nearby city, which suggested it must be quite late. The street out front was lined with similar old rag-tag mansions, and he noted nothing that might indicate he was near the river. The backyard seemed more hopeful, for there was no parallel road, just a scrubby decline peppered by nondescript trees. When he descended a ways, he paused because—

Yes!

—he heard water slowly moving over shallow rocks, and the redolence that came to his nostrils he would easily describe as "rivery." Another forty yards in descent, and he was standing on the river shore, and as luck would have it, here was a rowboat tied off on a small pier.

He looked across the dark, shimmering water with the gibbous face of the moon reflected in it, and there it was, just a dark, inchoate bump at first, but as his eyes grew accustomed to the twilight, Lovecraft's infamous island appeared. Everard couldn't remember ever having been in a rowboat, but he didn't hesitate to get in and start rowing this one toward the island.

A fog rolled in along the Miskatonic River, at times shrouding the island until a dank-smelling gust of wind pushed it out of shape and out of the way. Everard was indolently soft, and rowing was hard work, but he distracted himself by imagining different humiliating and violent ways in which he could exact revenge on the bitch who had sent him here. The one which initially pleased him was cutting into those massive tits like two Christmas hams. Another was shoving one of those polyhedrons far up into her—

A low pulsing sound distracted him from his vengeful thoughts, a kind of tinny heartbeat that was regularly irregular, a pattern of some sort, maybe. The moon had come out full and bright, but its light had a violet tinge to it that made him uneasy, and when he caught glimpses of the island through the fog, the tips of the long grasses seemed vaguely luminescent with the color. That didn't bother him nearly as much as the sound, though, which seemed to drag across his brain. It had all the pleasantness of chewing on tinfoil or biting into ice or listening to nails on a chalkboard or dragging a cheese grater across one's testicles, or—

Everard stopped rowing and shook his head. Where had *that* come from? His thoughts, even his limbs, felt alien to him, not entirely under his control, and that scared the shit out of him. The lapping of the water around the boat drew his attention to the fact that it was still moving, even though he wasn't rowing anymore, and that it was moving with *purpose*. All around him, inside his head as well as in his ears, he heard the sound coalescing. Now, it sounded like... like piping—flute piping, he thought.

In Lovecraft's work, the dreams were all part of the lure of the Black Man, an avatar of Nyarlathotep—his Big Book, the promises of the old crone and rat-like monstrosity as they dragged Walter Gilman across the space-time continuum and into other dimensions...

They had wanted Walter Gilman to go with them to see Azathoth, the blind idiot god of all things, on his black throne in the void of Chaos at the center of all universes.

Azathoth... Everard shuddered.

Of all the things that Everard had seen and felt and experienced in the hellish otherscapes of this crazy trip, the idea that Azathoth might, in any way, actually *exist* terrified him more than anything else. He was not one to readily give Lovecraft credit for much, but he had one more than one occasion thought, during his research into Lovecraft's mythology, that the one disturbing concept Lovecraft had foisted on readers of his rambling, melodramatic nonsense was that of Azathoth. Everard found the God of Christianity terrifying enough, and that Being was supposed to be not only all-knowing, but infinitely loving, as well. Azathoth neither knew nor cared about anything in all of its creation across multiple universes. It went on and on, lulled by the piping and the drumming of unnamed entities, dreaming all that is, was, and will be into actuality. To Azathoth, though, none of it was autonomous or significant in any way. It was no more important to the cosmic creature than the dream Everard had had last night was to him. Hell,

Everard barely even remembered his dreams upon waking.

What would happen to this universe and his own universe if that piping and drumming stopped? Worse, why was it so close, so near to Everard now that it filled his head? What if he accidentally did something that stopped the pipers and the drummers, and he somehow undid the whole of... everything?

He finally passed beneath the Miskatonic Bridge and the boat maneuvered itself toward a long, thin mound of land overgrown with marsh grasses. It silently approached the shore and slid onto the beach, then stopped. Cautiously, Everard got out of the boat.

At first glance, it was pretty much what he expected, based on the scant description in the story. He hadn't expected to find any houses on the island and was not surprised that he didn't see any.

He wasn't supposed to find people, either. That, he wasn't so sure would hold true.

The piping had grown louder, and now he could hear deep drumming that sounded like it was coming from the center of the island, deep in the earth. It was starting to get to him, messing with other sounds, making them alternately too loud or too soft for what normal, sane nature had designed them to be. He saw shadows flickering in the distance, taking shape and then distorting it. If they were people, he didn't want to know. He'd almost rather deal with Joe Sargeant and his big fish cock than meet whoever moved like those shadows did.

He took a deep breath and tried to summon some intestinal fortitude. For fuck's sake, the plan was simple enough, and he wasn't about to complicate it with worrying over stupid shadows now. He had to find the Decagon and get the hell out of there... while there was still a "there" to get the hell out of.

The wind had largely swept away the fog on the island—he could see for a few hundred yards ahead—and pushed it off to the river. When Everard glanced back, he could barely make the boat out on the coastline and could see nothing of Arkham beyond. It didn't matter, though, so long as the stone was there on the island. He would be winging his way to Dunwich soon enough, he supposed.

Unless Asenath had lied to him. That was a strong possibility.

He trudged toward the center of the island, sure somehow that this was the way he was supposed to go...or the way that the forces on the island wanted him to go.

In the story, Keziah Mason had appeared to Walter Gilman once on the island, but in every other "dream," the hapless youth had, she had taken him to what Lovecraft strongly suggested was the attic of the old house. It was there that the Black Man had shown Walter the book and Brown Jenkin had bitten his wrist. It was there that the baby had been... or would be, he supposed... sacrificed on Walpurgis Night. Was that tonight? Asenath had said something about Keziah being 300 years old at the time in which he had landed here, so that meant it was before Walter had confronted her and tried to stop the May-Eve ritual. Was that what was happening now, in that old house, while Walter thought he slept?

If so, that meant Keziah, Brown Jenkin, and Nyarlathotep were busy elsewhere. Maybe his luck would be in just once, and he would find the Decahedron unguarded, just waiting for him.

He glanced back in the direction he'd come and found he couldn't see the boat, or the coastline, for that matter, at all. He reminded himself once again that it was okay; he wouldn't need either if he found the stone.

When he focused again on the way ahead, he became aware of a faint amber glow, like an old lantern, coming from between a copse of tangled, black-barked trees. There, the shadows leaped and danced. The piping and drumming seemed to be coming from there, as well.

Cautiously, he crept closer, imaging the night gaunts and imps and ghouls that Lovecraft had populated the background of his stories with. If it was, indeed, Walpurgis night, those things had been called out of the bowels of the earth and places further and more infernal still. As if to reinforce his notion, a smell hit him that was both animal and sexual, a stale mix of blood and semen and the coppery scent of blood.

He ducked behind a thick, unnaturally twisting trunk and peered around it, squinting at the bright yellow-amber light that poured from a clearing just beyond.

His first thought came with relief—the Decahedron was there! It hung suspended about six feet off the ground from black vines whose origin disappeared into the mottled canopy overhead. Its facets glowed from some golden light beneath the surface. Its silver veins streaked erratically over the stone, casting odd shadows to dance across the clearing and its inhabitants as they blocked the light from within.

The second thought followed fairly quickly on the heels of the first as he took in the revelers and the scene before him, and the relief immediately dried up.

Circling the stone was a large ring of colorless fire that snapped and waved upward. It gave off no smoke and, so far as he could tell under the piping, made no crackling sound, though he could feel the heat of it as far back as he was. Between the ring of fire and the stone was debauchery the likes of which Everard could barely process.

The revelers around the stone were, indeed, non-human things, some of them humanoid or approximating human heads and limbs, winged like bats and possessed of countless horns in an assortment of patterns all over their bodies. Others looked like jellyfish with barbed tendrils that entwined and prodded and invaded the soft undersides of each other, while others looked like massive maggots made of jellied eyes and long, bony, curving teeth. Some were impossible to determine a shape for at all. It was hard to get any real sense of detail because the creatures were writhing all over each other, pulsing and pumping and winking in and out of view with the beating of the drums. Some plunged spike-ringed tentacles into

the dank, dripping chasms of others, sending shud-
ders through mounds of unidentifiable flesh and
gushing, fetid fluids from the chasms themselves.
Some sucked at the slimy, glistening appendages of
others. He saw a creature that looked like a hovering
giant string of breasts with an eye where each of the
nipples should have been. The winged things, partly
humanoid and partly insectoid, were rutting with
each other and then tearing into the flesh of their
partners and devouring them upon climax.

One creature which looked like a cross between
an ape and a shark lay beneath it, waving tentacles
from where the hands or fins should have been. A
tentacle squeezed one of the breasts nearly to burst-
ing, then plunged itself deep into the iris, which
seemed to shudder and moan and pulse greedily for
the rest of the tentacle's length.

Everard saw another long appendage shooting
out from a cloud of eyes, ringed with thousands and
thousands of very human-looking fingers. He
watched the appendage rip at something that looked
like a tree with quivering bark-crusted labia, tearing
bits of the bark away to expose slick white flesh. The
tentacle then dove into the hole between the lip and
began pumping and thrusting, and the tree-thing
gyrated, moaning and calling out in a language
Everard didn't know, but was sure was a string of
obscene commands.

The stench was awful this close, hitting him in
waves full in the face. It reminded him of unclean
things—disease and oozing pus, the stink of
sweating flanks and animal lust, the nauseating smell

of rot being ejaculated onto the desperate fleshy surfaces of others.

That wasn't the worst of it, though.

Those who weren't fucking and feasting on non-human partners partook, it seemed, of an assortment of body parts that had once been human. These were laid out on a long stone slab near the back of the orgy. Everard recognized a few disarticulated limbs, but mostly, he saw naked heads and torsos, armless and legless, which the monstrosities swooped over and tore meaty chunks out of or lifted and carried off to penetrate any number of orifices available. Some of those mutilated and partial bodies were *still alive*, still writhing in pain and bleeding from their stringy, shredded stumps and wailing as an assortment of probing, monstrous appendages invaded bloody mouths, rectums, and vaginas. Mercifully, the first few thrusts seemed to daze if not kill them outright. Those not devoured after were returned to the slab, in whole or as dismembered torsos and heads, for the next reveler to use.

Some of the torsos were small... very small.

He saw hideous imp-like things dancing around the orgy, flapping and dragging their own distorted limbs, shrieking and moaning in time with the piping.

Shit, Everard thought, tearing his eyes away from the horrors to focus on the glowing stone in their center. *How the hell am I going to get to it? I'll be eaten alive.*

He considered waiting the monsters out; after all, how long could they go? Even if their appetites were inexhaustible, the sun had to come up sometime, and that would surely put an end to their revels. He glanced around him uneasily, feeling an acute vulnerability in having his back to the vast darkness of the island. To wait would be taking a risk, even if not as big a risk as charging into the fray toward the stone. Action or inaction, either way, could render him a limbless fucktoy/dinner for those monstrosities cavorting in the clearing if any one of them discovered he was there.

He could just imagine Asenath's smug pleasure at his being in this situation, and he flushed with heated anger.

A twig snapping behind him made him jump and spin around, but he managed not to cry out. He searched the illimitable darkness but of course, he saw nothing. A giggle came out of the black, high-pitched and thin, and his skin crawled. This was followed a moment later by a low growl which seemed to reverberate between the trees.

What he'd seen in the clearing was horrific. It occurred to him, though, that what could be out there in the darkness waiting for him could be worse.

Turning back to the moaning and screeching of the clearing, he took a deep breath. Before he realized what he was doing, he was running...

Running and darting around snapping tentacles and quivering, gelatinous masses, ducking under flailing limbs and talons swiping the air, running and jumping over gyrating flesh and puddles of stinking, blue-black ichor, crimson blood, and pearlescent fluids he refused to allow himself to think about. The creature's bodies were nauseating this close, nearly knocking him down with their overpowering sour reek and moving parts. He thought he heard the torsos on the stone slab and smothering beneath inhuman bodies calling to him, begging, pleading with him to just kill them, kill them, but he ignored them. He couldn't stop, not even for a moment, not until—

He was standing under the stone, a single calm eye in the storm of atrocities. He gazed up into it, hoping it would kick in before anything else in the clearing reached him. As he tried to forget what was happening around him, to lose himself in the glow of the stone, he felt what his brain processed as a thousand tiny needles dragged down his back and over his ass. The limb touching him seemed to split apart, one branch snaking its way down his pants and between his legs while the other sank its multitude of needles into his shoulder. The pain threatened to pull his concentration away from the stone, but he persisted.

Gold, gold light, light, striations, gold light—

Another branch wound its way around the unimpressive length of his dick—

Deeper, deeper into the light, the gold light, the silver streaks winding around his mind—

Something was tearing at him, at parts of him beneath his waist and along his shoulder blade—

The gold and silver dazzled, tore away the darkness, and the sensation of needles sinking into his testicles faded away—

The light got brighter, brighter, until it filled his eyes, filled all things, surrounded him, lifted him, pushed away all that was around him, and he was moving, moving—

The light vanished.

The piping faded into an echo, although the drumming persisted for several minutes after. The latter might have been Everard's heartbeat, though, a quick, dull thudding. There was no pain, and in fact, no sensation at all, except for a cold that sank beneath his flesh, slipped under his muscles, and settled in his bones. He couldn't see himself in the void around him, a night deeper than that of the island and unfathomably vast. He knew it to be space, but there were no stars. No planets, no moons, no comets, no nebulae, no swirling gases or explosions. This was the edge of space, the place where stars had died or were never born, the oldest corners where nothing was or would be, not even the most ancient and basic elements of the cosmos.

Of all that he had seen, of all that remained in his conscious and subconscious minds, this scared him the most. This was the undoing of creation, the place of no more and never was. This was Azathoth awakening, shaking off its musings of the universe, no longer lulled into dreams of creation.

Nothing had ever made him feel so small, so insignificant, so non-existent. In the void, there was only madness without form or end.

Then, even consciousness abandoned him, and darkness swallowed all.

Whether that lasted a single second, as Everard perceived it, or a billion relentless years, was beyond Everard's comprehension. The next thing he was aware of was waking up on a bale of hay, with straw sticking into his shoulder and crotch and the heavy, almost overpowering animal reek still in his nostrils. Darkness surrounded him like a hot, humid breath.

He stood on shaky legs, the echoes of pain that almost was like an aftertouch on his body. As his eyes adjusted to the gloom around him, he made out wooden beams and stacks of hay bales, as well as the amorphous shapes of rotting things close to the door.

Cows, he thought sourly. *If I really have made it to Dunwich, this will be the wizard Whateley's old barn where he kept the cows that he was feeding to—*

He caught a whiff of ozone above the animal and rot smells, and he frowned. The smell was quickly followed by a snapping, crunching sound which, given the ozone, Everard took to be thunder. A storm was coming, possibly.

In Lovecraft's story, a ring of stones atop the rounded hill outside served as a location for the Whateley's rituals, and as the final battleground between Wilbur Whateley's twin brother and the men of Arkham University. It was most likely there that Everard would find the last stone— the Hexakosihexekontahexagon, the stone—he hoped—that would take him back to the hotel in Williamsburg, back to his own time and his own reality. If he could make it there without getting torn apart or devoured by the monstrous son of Yog-Sothoth...

Everard moved toward the barn doors and the pile of what he could now make out as bones and offal from the cows Whateley kept buying. Up this close, the smell was nauseating, and he turned his head and gave the mess a wide berth as he inched his way around to the doors.

He gave one door a disgusted push and was surprised to find it only gave a little. Through the small crack in the parting doors, he could see that they were barred with heavy wooden timber.

"Son of a bitch," he muttered to himself, glancing around the barn. There was a loft overhead, but no ladder to reach it that he could see, nor did there appear to be anything in the way of tools he could use to break the boards.

He kicked the door hard and cursed again. This place—

A cracking outside got his attention, followed by a ground-shaking thud, and then another. The ozone smell grew stronger, mixing with the noxiousness of the barn air.

Everard held his breath.

The ground shook again, closer. *Footsteps?*

Everard put his ear to the door, listening. The sounds were coming this way, toward the barn.

He backed away, stumbling over the cow viscera as his eyes remained fixed on the door.

There was a creaking sound, like something outside was leaning on the wood, and then a terrible crack as the doors caved in. In fact, the whole front of the barn came with it, and several supporting beams, too. Everard dove behind a bale of hay as the roof of the barn was torn off by unseen hands and tossed aside. Early morning sun slanted toward what was left of the barn and a strong animal-ozone smell dropped heavily in its place. Everard looked around.

It wasn't just the roof, but the walls, as well, and from his nakedly vulnerable place behind a hay bale, he could see that it was not only the barn, but the sheds that Whateley had fixed up for him and Wilbur and Lavinia to live in once the creature got too big to confine to the upstairs of their house. Everard could see what was left of their foundations poking up out of the grass beyond the muddy road. In fact, most of the house, he saw, was gone, too.

Heavy marks the size of barrels led away from the property and along the road by a glen toward the village. It had escaped. The creature that Lavinia Whateley had given birth to was loose in Dunwich.

"Think," Everard muttered to himself. "Just think." In Lovecraft's story, the creature had broken out of the Whateley farmhouse the night of September 9th and had gone on its rampage of destruction around Dunwich the next day. The men from Arkham—Armitage, Rice, and Morgan—would be on their way, having read Wilbur's diary and the books kept as part of "his larnin.'" They would meet with the monster on Sentinel Hill and banish it back where it came from.

But not yet—not before it managed to take out a bunch of farmhouses and the families inside them. And while it was busy, he could make his way up the hill and get to the stone.

He felt a twinge of guilt for the families in the creature's wake; men, women, and children just *gone*, just wiped off the earth... or this reality's version of it, anyway. Realistically, though, there was nothing he could do. Maybe there was nothing he *should* do. Who knew what would happen if he did something to actually change the narrative of Lovecraft's work.

He ran across the grass and started up the hill, his eyes darting around to make sure no one and nothing was following. He didn't want to have to explain himself to these half-inbred yokels about who he was and why he was heading toward the haunted standing stones on top of Sentinel Hill.

The way Lovecraft had described it, Everard had imagined an almost cartoonishly rounded hill, not the steep, curving slope he slogged up with ragged breaths. He was once again painfully aware that he needed to get out and exercise more.

As he pulled himself up the final slope of the hill, he saw the ring of standing stones. They were smooth and grayish-green like polished soapstone, somewhat obelisk-shaped, and stood about eight or nine feet tall. Deep marks had been carved on the surfaces facing inward; they appeared to have some pattern to them, but they were unlike any kind of hieroglyphs or runes Everard had ever seen.

So here I am, he thought in a daze. *I'm standing on the top of Lovecraft's Sentinel Hill...*

Within the center of the stones was a massive slab of the same composition, roughly hewn into a rectangular block with a smooth top. It stood chest-high to Everard, who noted myriad dark brownish stains on its expansive surface.

But at first he noticed nothing else substantial about the slab.

A massive thunderclap exploded overhead, which toppled Everard and landed him on his back. If he'd eaten more food the day before, he easily would've crapped in his pants.

Motherfucker! he thought, and then a second clap detonated, even louder than the first, and down the slope of the hill, a lightning bolt clove a massive oak tree in half. The strike turned his surroundings into a one-second flash of full daylight. *Fuck this shit!* But should he run for cover? A frantic glance overhead revealed no signs of any storm, just a still silent moon —gibbous—three-quarters full.

Trembling, he dragged himself up.

"It was here all along," came a soft, exotic voice— a woman's voice. "You're just not very attentive. Is something... distracting you?"

It was Asenath's voice. "But you couldn't see it..."

Everard stared, all thoughts of the Hexakosihex-ekontahexagon brushed aside.

It was her, here, in the flesh.

The grinning witch sat lewd and naked atop the sacrificial slab. Grinning and spread-legged. Her flawless white skin glowed as lambently as the moonlight.

10

Everard should've been thinking about anything besides Asenath's nude body. The robust physique was almost otherworldy in its perfection, its curvatures the epitome of male lust. *Tits to die for,* he crudely thought, unable to refrain from staring at them, each the size of a duckpin ball, sagless, with jutting dark pink nipples. This was, indeed, biological flawlessness, save for—

Everard gagged and thought *Vandalism!*

Asenath's well-toned arms and legs were besmirched by untold Lovecraft tattoos.

Fuck me. But... I'll do her anyway...

"Fuckin-A," Everard croaked. "Wish I could say I'm happy to see you..."

"Oh, you'll be happy," she intoned. "Because I'm your deliverer. You've passed your penance, Professor Everard. I would've bet that you would have died a minute after setting foot in the Church of Starry

Wisdom, but I'm delighted to see I was wrong. Very few have lived to tell *this* tale. Bravo."

"'It must be allow'd,'" Asenath began, "'that these Blasphemies of an infernall Train of Daemons are Matters of a too common Knowledge to be deny'd.' That's a quote, Professor. Do you remember who spoke those words?"

Everard did. "Reverend Abijah Hoadley, the parson of the Dunwich Congregational Church. He disappeared shortly after delivering that sermon in 1747."

"He disappeared, all right, and trust me, you don't want to know the details of that disappearance."

"I'll take your word for it." He forced himself to look at her eyes instead of her raving body. "Where's the stone?"

"The stone?" She giggled. "Oh, do you mean the Hexakosihexekontahexagon?"

"Yeah. *That* stone. I can't pronounce the mother-fucker. You just said it was here, but I couldn't see it. It's invisible like Wilbur's twin?"

"No, no. It's been here the whole time. Like Poe's 'Purloined Letter,' it's inconspicuous even in plain sight." She picked up something minuscule off the slab: a half-inch-square metal box with its lip flipped open. Her magnificent breasts dipped when she leaned forward and placed the tiny box in his hand.

You gotta be kidding me... The tiny metal box was very similar to the much larger one that encased the Shining Trapezohedron back at the church, and inside there was indeed a gemstone, but it was only the size of a chickpea. Of course he hadn't seen it—it was tiny while he'd expected the biggest polyhedron yet. This one, small as it was, shone in a luminous forest green, highlighted by threadlike striations of molten gold.

"It was on this same sacrificial plinth," the macabre woman went on, "that Yog-Sothoth impregnated Lavinia Whateley on May Eve, 1912. The poor woman was severely stricken by genetic defects due to inbreeding, but she was all Wizard Whateley had to offer. A more perfect union would've provided for a perfect offspring,"

"So I presume Wilbur is dead now," Everard stated.

"Um-hmm. Torn to pieces by the guard dog at the Miskatonic Library, where he came very close to procuring the proper translation of page 751 of the English version of the Necronomicon. If he'd succeeded, your world and our world would've been cleared of all human life by now, readying itself for the return of its true kings. What a pity."

"And his twin brother? He's gone now as well?"

"Not quite yet." Asenath grinned lasciviously. She took back the tiny box and put it aside on the slab, and then parted her legs more obscenely. "You better make it quick if you're gonna do it. Wilbur's brother is coming..."

Everard looked down the hillside and saw trees collapsing in a line. Some unseen force was flattening them as more thunder rumbled from the black swirls over fast-moving clouds. Something screeched in the air from miles off, and concussions like rapid, unearthly footfalls seemed to be gaining on Sentinel Hill.

"Wait'll you see it!" Asenath whispered, her eyes beaming.

"Nobody can see it!" Everard yelled, recalling the story. "It's in another dimension! It's invisible!"

"Not this close to the plinth..."

Everard continued to stare desperately over his shoulder while Asenath wrapped her bare legs around him from where she sat on the slab. Her hands pulled him closer, then began fumbling with his belt.

Everard wasn't exactly in the mood, not as some massive extraterrestrial juggernaut thudded closer and closer. He kept trying to pull away and Asenath kept pulling him back into her. "Get your cock out! Quick! This is what you've wanted since the minute we met. Another piece of ass, another notch for your gun," and then she threw her head back and laughed, her breasts practically in his face.

But he was paying the situation no mind.

A crackling reared up behind him, along with the sense that something hillock-sized was straining to materialize. Bolts of lightning divided and subdivided into particles like metallic dust around a magnet. Everard squinted as that ozone smell returned, but instead of the admixture of organic rot, it chaperoned something infinitely more noxious yet indescribable. Then, almost like a fade-in pixelation, Wilbur Whateley's twin brother phase-shifted into view...

"Awesome, isn't he?" Asenath said.

The sudden appearance of a semi-phosphorescent excrescence dissolved into view, throbbing with gobs of sharper light, like sparklers, the color of snot. But from within that, there appeared a percolating, office-building-sized mass with a center that made Everard think of a titanic jellyfish, but whose extremities more resembled writhing earthworms over a hundred feet long but the width of suspension-bridge cables. At the end of these lower extremities were VW-Bug-sized things like cloven hoofs. The upper extremities terminated with things like huge human hands but with six or seven fingers each.

Then came the head, which more resembled *two* heads mashed together. Something akin to half a malformed human face occupied one side of the massive bump: two great lop-sided eyes pushed together, with yellow irises, topped by yellowish crinkly hair. Quivering maroon lips and a collapsed nose. This component of the "face" had one most obvious feature—it had inherited the Whateley chin-lessness and the off-yellow, hugely pored skin.

But then there came the other half of this facsimile for a head: a visage wholly apart from anything the known material universe could produce, something from somewhere else, a place that shared virtually nothing with the physical and biological laws that humans could comprehend...

The rapid thuds described the thing's awkward ascent up Sentinel Hill. The earth shook such that Everard feared the whole of the eminence might collapse; he was encased by a tenor of fear unlike anything he'd known, not just the calamity of earth-shaking concussion but being able to see the actual entity that caused it. His eyes riveted to the thing's thorax, mid-section, center-of-mass, or whatever it might be called, and he gazed hypnotized at the various organic integrants within, an unworldly, oscillating mound of gelatinous slurry somehow held together by psychics beyond modern comprehension.

Then the monstrosity's mouth opened, a semi-cosmic aperture on the "Wilbur-half" of the impossible face. Everard knew one thing: *I don't want to go in that...*

One of those garage-door-sized six-fingered human hands began to reach down...

"Time for you to go, Professor," Asenath said in a sing-songy voice.

He looked down, one last time, at the woman's perfect breasts and body—

She pulled her knees back to her chin and slammed her feet against his chest with surprising jackhammer force.

Everard didn't remember if he was screaming or not; nevertheless, he was shot propulsively away from the stone slab and, end over end, he began to tumble down the slope of Sentinel Hill. Above him, an explosion cracked out, but he knew at once it was a howl of objection exploding from the throat of Wilbur Whateley's twin brother.

Everard rolled and rolled; it was like getting run over by a car, but by the time his body got to the bottom of the hill—

He was no longer there.

11

Everard saw only black; he was immersed in a lightless domain with no perceptible boundaries, and he heard nothing save for a steady annoying beeping sound that seemed perfectly aligned to the beat of his heart. It occurred to him that his only course of action would be to follow the beeping...

Where the hell am I? Am I dead?

Wherever he was, he knew it was no longer Sentinel Hill.

Moments later, the blackness bled out of his vision, and to his dismay, he found himself lying in a hospital bed with an I.V. in one arm, a blood pressure cuff, and heart monitor sensors stuck to his chest.

Opened curtains to his left showed him it was nighttime, and a clock revealed the time—just past midnight.

"Oh, there he is," came a woman's voice. He was

thrilled that it wasn't Asenath's. "How are you feeling?"

"I..."

"You're in Riverside Doctor's Hospital, and you're going to be okay."

Everard's vision cleared; a nurse stood next to him, a generic, middle-aged brunette with a typical nurse's cap.

"What city am I in?"

The nurse's eyes thinned. "Williamsburg, Virginia. Don't you remember being here? They found you unconscious over the big hill. It looks like you passed out when you were coming back from the tourist village.

I was in another dimension, lady. Not a tourist village... "What's wrong with me?"

"Dr. Houghton says you're experiencing an acute distress disorder." She laid a comforting hand on his arm. "It's a mild form of shock and will dissipate soon. You're a little dehydrated and your labs indicate some malnutrition."

That's right, I never ate or drank anything when I was over there, he realized. *I could've been there for days.*

"But we'll have you back to rights in no time. You'll have to stay the night, though," said the nurse. "You'll need a few more tests, and you have a nasty bruise on your head. Did you fall down?"

He looked right at her. "I fell down, all right." *I fell down a hill with a para-dimensional monster on it.* "But I feel pretty good, and no, I wasn't drinking."

The nurse smiled, writing on a clipboard. "What

brings you to Williamsburg, if you don't mind me asking?"

Everard swallowed. "I was a guest speaker at a fan convention. H.P. Lovecraft, if you know who he was."

The nurse's handwriting stopped, and she looked at him as if in shock herself. "Were you staying at the Double Tree Hotel?"

"Why, yes."

Silence. Then, "My God. Do you know what happened?"

"Happened?" he asked. "No, what happened?" But he had a sinking feeling in this gut, even before she turned on the TV.

Holy shit...

"... remain mystified by the event," a stern female newscaster was saying, "and are still unsure of the definite cause. At approximately 9:30 p.m. Eastern Standard Time, the Williamsburg Double Tree Hotel was destroyed in a catastrophe that police authorities have suggested was a terrorist bomb or a major eruption of natural gas lines. James City County Fire Chief Allen Barlow has suggested that some kind of chemical corrosive may have come into play, due to burns and malformations of some of the decedents..."

Everard stared at the TV screen, jaw hanging. In a rolling news clip, the entirety of the hotel sat collapsed, as if crushed, with smoke billowing hundreds of feet into the air. At least a dozen fire trucks had responded, their crews struggling to extinguish relentless flames. The newscaster's voice grimly continued, "Thus far, no survivors have been found, and it is feared that over a thousand convention attendees may have perished. The following footage is very graphic and not suitable for sensitive viewers..."

Everard's jaw dropped down another notch as the next clips panned over swaths of smoking rubble. Charred corpses could easily be seen, some with malformed bones that seemed bowed and yellowed. "Slightly elevated levels of radiation have also been detected..."

A wider shot showed the entire demolished hotel; its surrounding property was encircled by a calamity of fire trucks, ambulances, police, and flashing lights, while droves of rescue workers exited the fringes of the debris bearing covered black-stained stretchers, some still smoking.

"Awful, isn't it?" the nurse remarked. "Maybe even a terrorist bombing, they said. My God, who would do such a thing?"

Everard's brain was ticking madly, and the wildest theories entered his head. "Looks like I lucked out. I had a room in that hotel. If I'd been inside..."

The nurse grimaced. "Thank the Fates you weren't." She lowered her clipboard. "I have to go back on my rounds now, so just buzz if you need anything. The doctor should be along shortly."

"Thank you."

"And here's your cellphone in case you want to make any calls." She reached into a plastic bag labeled PATIENT PROPERTY, then passed him his phone.

He nodded, still thinking, and she left the room. *In case I want to make any calls...*

But as he considered this, the phone—unmelted, it seemed—rang. UNKNOWN NUMBER.

"What the hell did you do?" he demanded.

"I didn't really do anything," Aseneth half-laughed. "You did it all yourself."

"Something destroyed the whole hotel!"

"Have you looked in your pants pocket?"

My fuckin' pants pocket?

Everard groaned and jumped off the bed. He stumbled over to the property bag, pulled out his pants, and in his back pocket found—

No...

He withdrew the tiny metal box housing the minuscule Hexakosihexekontahexagon. The lid was closed; he flipped it back open.

He knew then that it was no terrorist bomb that had demolished the hotel.

His feet dragged across the cold floor as he returned to his phone. "You still there?"

"Yes, indeed. Good work, Professor. Now you know the real power of what's going on here, the same power that Lovecraft revealed so long ago. But don't worry, it takes a while for the stone to reset." A chuckle. "Just keep the lid open."

"You slipped that fucking thing in my pocket while—"

"—while your attention was distracted by the body you were lusting for, yes. You're quite the inter-dimensional courier! You should get a bonus!"

"A thousand people may have died here, you psycho witch!"

"It'll be a lot more than a thousand one day very soon. Maybe a million, maybe a *billion*. I'm glad you've gotten the opportunity to see the ancient truth of the Haunter of the Dark. You're quite privileged to be a part of this."

Privileged, Everard thought, nauseous. "Fuck you."

"And you can use the stone to come back here anytime you want—"

"Like hell I will!" Everard shouted at her. "There's something seriously fucked up with you."

"Or if you won't come to me, maybe I'll come to you."

With that, Everard nearly threw up.

"One way or another," Asenath went on, "you can count on it. We'll meet again. In fact, I'm really looking forward to it—"

click

Everard stood in place for some minutes, unblinking, his heart chugging slowly. In his mind, he thought he could hear a multitude of people screaming as they were burned alive, and he sensed more than saw something black, immense, and immaterial drift out of existence. But eventually and without much awareness, he shuffled over to the big window and found himself gazing out into the limitless twilight. A squashed, yellow moon hung suspended there, a *gibbous* moon.

His phone blipped.

Numb now, he made his eyes flick down to the

screen and he saw that Asenath had texted him a single, stolid jpeg: a black and white portrait of the face of H.P. Lovecraft.

END

ACKNOWLEDGMENTS

Mary would like to thank her husband Brian Keene, her daughter Ada, and the SanGiovanni/Serra and Keene families for their love and support, Christoph and Leza for their hard work and faith in our book, Paul Goblirsch at Thunderstorm Books for his friendship and general awesomeness, and of course, Ed Lee, for exploring new dimensions of the written word with me.

ABOUT EDWARD LEE

Edward Lee is the author of over 50 horror novels, and dozens of short stories. He has also had comic scripts published by DC Comics, Verotik Inc., and Cemetery Dance. Many of his novels have been reprinted in other countries. He has won multiple awards for his fiction and a Lifetime Achievement Award in 2020. The movie version of his novella HEADER is now available on Tubi; his collaborative script (with David C. Hayes), OUIJA SLUMBER PARTY, recently sold to SRS Cinema.

ABOUT MARY SANGIOVANNI

Mary SanGiovanni is an award-winning American horror and thriller writer of nearly two dozen novels and novellas, including her most recent media tie-in novel for the *Alien* franchise, *Enemy of My Enemy*, her fan-favorite Kathy Ryan series, and *For Emmy*, soon to me made into a film. She has also written short stories, comics for Marvel and DC, and non-fiction. She has a Masters degree in Writing Popular Fiction from Seton Hill University, Pittsburgh. She has the distinction of being one of the first women to speak about writing at the CIA Headquarters in Langley, VA, and offers talks and workshops on writing around the country. Born and raised in New Jersey, she currently resides in Pennsylvania.

ALSO BY CLASH BOOKS

THE PINK AGAVE MOTEL

V. Castro

GIGANTVM PENISIVM

Jose Elvin Bueno

SELENE SHADE: RESURRECTIONIST FOR HIRE

Victoria Dalpe

THE KING OF VIDEO POKER

Paolo Iacovelli

INVAGINIES

Joe Koch

CATHERINE THE GHOST

Kathe Koja

EVERYTHING THE DARKNESS EATS

Eric LaRocca

THE BODY HARVEST

Michael J. Seidlinger

FLOWERS FROM THE VOID

Gianni Washington

H O R R O R

WE PUT THE LIT IN LITERARY

CLASHBOOKS.COM

FOLLOW US

IG

X

@clashbooks

TikTok

@clashbook